His ENCORE Her ECSTASY

An Age Gap Romance

TRISHA FUENTES

Published by
Ardent Artist Books
www.ardentartistbooks.com

about ardent artist books

Follow us on YouTube!
https://bit.ly/3W3xn7a

Like, Subscribe & Comment

* * *

➡ <u>WE HAVE SERIALIZED FICTION!</u>

Visit our website today to download one of our stories
that unfold in bite-sized pieces!

Each installment is just 99¢!

https://bit.ly/3LsDpJL

* * *

➡ <u>LET'S CONNECT!</u>

**Fuel your love of fiction with exclusive content and
captivating insights from Ardent Artist Books.**
Whether you crave the thrill of modern narratives or the
timeless elegance of historical fiction, our newsletter
delivers a curated selection straight to your inbox. Plus, as
a welcome gift, receive a FREE downloadable eBook:

"The Family Fix"

https://bit.ly/49BR3UB

contents

one

. . .

Olympia, Washington

Charlotte ran her fingers along the spines of the books, their worn covers like old friends. She inhaled the musty scent, a calming ritual that marked the start of each day.

"Lottie, you really need to join this century," Cassie called from the front counter. "No one uses the Dewey Decimal System anymore."

Charlotte smiled as she slid a yellowed copy of *"The Great Gatsby"* into its proper place. "There's beauty in order, Cass. Besides, I like the classics."

Cassie leaned on the counter, red curls tumbling over her shoulders. "Speaking of classics, Jake's band is playing at The Lounge tonight. Very retro rock vibe. We should go!"

Charlotte hesitated. Socializing didn't come easily to her, even with Cassie's infectious enthusiasm pulling her along. "I don't know... I was planning to reorganize the poetry section tonight."

Cassie stared at her friend like she had three eyes in the center of her head. "You've got to be kidding me. You can fondle your precious books anytime!" Cassie sauntered over, hips swinging. She plucked the stack of novels from Charlotte's hands. "When's the last time you got out there and had some fun? Maybe met a guy, blew off some steam?"

Heat crept up Charlotte's neck at the insinuation. Casual hook-ups weren't really her style. She preferred imagining the dalliances within her fiction - all the yearning and desire, without the messy vulnerability of real life.

Still, Cassie's words needled at her. *Was she missing out, nose perpetually buried in a book? A night of live music did sound freeing.* And maybe it was time to let someone past the walls she'd so carefully constructed...

"Okay, fine." Charlotte sighed, no match for Cassie's persuasive powers. "I'll come tonight. But I'm not making any promises about meeting guys!"

Cassie squealed and pulled her into a hug. "Yes! It's going

to be epic. Who knows, maybe you'll find your Gatsby in the crowd." She winked.

Charlotte rolled her eyes, but couldn't suppress a grin. With Cassie by her side, she felt a flicker of the spontaneity she so admired in her literary heroines.

She turned back to the bookshelf, straightening the novels with renewed purpose. Tonight she would step into a story of her own making. And see where the evening's pages led her.

Just as Charlotte placed the last book on the shelf, the tinkle of the bell above the door signaled the arrival of a customer. She turned to greet them with a polite smile, but it quickly faded when she recognized the man who entered. It was Mr. Thompson, a regular known for his constant complaints and unreasonable demands.

"Excuse me, miss," he said gruffly, approaching the counter where Charlotte stood. "I bought this book here last week, and it's just not what I expected. I demand a refund."

Charlotte glanced at the book he held out, noting the creased spine and dog-eared pages. She took a deep breath, steeling herself for the inevitable confrontation.

"I apologize for the inconvenience, Mr. Thompson," she said calmly, her voice even and professional. "However, as stated in our return policy, we can only offer refunds on books returned in their original condition within seven days of purchase."

Mr. Thompson's face reddened, his brow furrowing in anger. "This is unacceptable! I've been a loyal customer for years, and this is how you treat me?"

Charlotte fought the urge to shrink back, instead meeting his gaze with quiet determination. She understood his frustration, but she also knew that bending the rules would only lead to more problems down the line.

"I truly am sorry, Mr. Thompson," she said, her tone gentle yet firm. "Perhaps we can find another book that better suits your interests? I'd be happy to make some recommendations."

For a moment, Mr. Thompson looked like he might argue further, but something in Charlotte's demeanor seemed to give him pause. His shoulders slumped, and he let out a defeated sigh.

"Fine," he grumbled, placing the book on the counter. "But I expect better service in the future."

"Of course, Mr. Thompson. I appreciate your understanding." Charlotte smiled, relief washing over her as the man turned and stalked out of the store.

She let out a long breath, her heart racing from the confrontation. Dealing with difficult customers was never easy, but she knew it was part of the job. And in a way, it was a challenge she relished - the opportunity to find common ground, to turn a negative experience into a positive one.

Just as she was about to return to her work, the shrill ring of the telephone pierced the air. Charlotte picked up the receiver, expecting it to be a customer inquiring about a book.

"Harmony Books, this is Charlotte speaking. How may I assist you?"

"Hello, is this Charlotte Madden?" a man's voice asked, his tone formal and professional.

"Yes, this is she. May I ask who's calling?"

"Ms. Madden, my name is Edward Larsen. I'm calling on behalf of the law firm Larsen & Associates. I regret to inform you that your grandmother, Evelyn Madden, has passed away."

Charlotte felt the air leave her lungs, her grip tightening on the phone. *Her grandmother?* She hadn't seen or heard from her so-called grandmother in over ten years. "I…I don't understand," she stammered, her mind reeling. "What happened? And why are you calling *me?*"

The lawyer cleared his throat, his voice softening with sympathy. "Ms. Madden, I know this must come as a shock. Your grandmother passed away peacefully in her sleep a few days ago. And the reason I'm calling is that she left you something in her will. A music venue called **The Velvet Room**."

Charlotte's eyes widened, her heart pounding in her chest. *A music venue? From my grandmother? A woman I never really knew? She was my father's mother, but when my father died—we lost touch.* Everlyn Madden was always a bit of a wild child, with an outgoing over-the-top personality—she could see her owning a music venue. *It was too much to process, too unexpected.*

She sank into the chair behind the counter, her legs suddenly weak. The lawyer was saying something about legal documents and next steps, but his words seemed to fade into the background as Charlotte's thoughts spun out of control.

What did this mean for her? For her life, her future? She had always found comfort in the familiar, in the routine of her days at the bookstore. But now, with this sudden inheritance, everything felt uncertain.

Charlotte took a shaky breath, trying to focus on the lawyer's voice. She knew she needed to deal with this, to face whatever lay ahead. But for now, all she could do was sit there, the phone pressed to her ear, and try to make sense of the bomb that had just been dropped on her carefully ordered world.

two days later

Charlotte stepped into the lawyer's office, her heart racing with a mix of anxiety and curiosity. The room was spacious and well-appointed, with rich mahogany furniture and floor-to-ceiling bookshelves. Sunlight streamed through the large windows, casting a warm glow across the space.

The lawyer, a middle-aged man with graying hair and kind eyes, greeted her with a sympathetic smile. "Ms. Madden, thank you for coming in. Please, have a seat."

Charlotte settled into the plush leather chair across from his desk, her hands clasped tightly in her lap. She tried to steady her breathing, but her mind was still reeling from the news of her grandmother's passing and the unexpected inheritance.

"I know this must be a difficult time for you," the lawyer said gently, pulling out a folder from his desk drawer. "Your grandmother, Evelyn, was a remarkable woman. **The Velvet Room** was her pride and joy."

He slid the folder across the desk toward Charlotte. "These are the legal documents pertaining to your inheritance. The music venue is yours now, along with a small sum of money to help with any necessary renovations or expenses."

Charlotte's fingers trembled slightly as she opened the folder, her eyes scanning the pages of legal jargon. She swallowed hard, trying to process the magnitude of what was happening.

"I... I don't understand," she said softly, her voice barely above a whisper. "Why would she leave this to *me*? We weren't close. I haven't seen her in years."

The lawyer leaned forward, his expression understanding. "Your grandmother always spoke highly of you, Ms. Madden. She admired your love for music and your appreciation for the arts. After the untimely passing of your father, Evelyn believed that you were the right person to carry on her legacy."

Charlotte felt a lump form in her throat, tears pricking at the corners of her eyes. She had always felt a sense of disconnect from her family, but knowing that her grandmother had thought of her, had believed in her... it was overwhelming.

"**The Velvet Room** was more than just a music venue to your grandmother," the lawyer continued. "It was a place where people could come together, where they could find solace and inspiration through music. She owned the entire building—there's even office space and a small apartment just above the bar and stage. She poured her heart and soul into that place, and she wanted to ensure that it would continue to thrive, even after she was gone."

Charlotte nodded slowly, her mind racing with possibilities and doubts. *Could she really do this? Could she take on the responsibility of running a music venue, of carrying on her grandmother's legacy?*

She took a deep breath, straightening her shoulders. She knew it wouldn't be easy, but something inside her, a flicker of determination and curiosity, urged her forward.

"Thank you," she said to the lawyer, her voice growing stronger. "I appreciate you taking the time to explain all of this to me. I... I think I need some time to process everything, but I want to honor my grandmother's wishes. I want to see what I can do with **The Velvet Room**."

The lawyer smiled, a glimmer of approval in his eyes. "I think your grandmother would be very proud of you, Ms. Madden. If you need anything, please don't hesitate to reach out. I'm here to help you navigate this new chapter in your life."

Charlotte left the lawyer's office with a sense of purpose, her mind already spinning with ideas and plans. She knew there would be challenges ahead, but for the first time in a long time, she felt a spark of excitement, a sense of possibility.

As she stepped out into the sunlit street, she couldn't help but feel a connection to her grandmother, a woman she had barely known but who had somehow seen something special in her. With a deep breath and a small smile, Charlotte began to walk, ready to embrace the unexpected journey that lay ahead.

CHARLOTTE RETURNED TO HARMONY BOOKS, the familiar chime of the bell above the door grounding her in the present. She moved through the aisles on autopilot, her fingers brushing against the spines of beloved books and vinyl records. The lawyer's words echoed in her mind, intertwined with distant memories of her grandmother's laughter and the faint strains of jazz.

Lost in thought, Charlotte nearly stumbled over a stack of books she had left on the floor earlier. She blinked, realizing that her usually meticulous organization had fallen by the wayside. With a sigh, she bent down to pick up the scattered volumes, her mind still consumed by the weight of her inheritance.

As she shelved the books, Charlotte's gaze drifted to the window, where the afternoon sun cast a warm glow over the street. She imagined **The Velvet Room** bathed in that same light, the stage awaiting the return of music and life. A flicker of excitement danced in her chest, tempered by the uncertainty of the unknown.

"What am I going to do?" she whispered to herself, her fingers tracing the worn edges of a vintage record sleeve. The thought of leaving the comfort of Harmony Books, of stepping into a world she barely knew, both thrilled and terrified her.

But as Charlotte looked around the store, at the carefully curated collection she had built over the years, she realized that her love for music and storytelling had always been a part of her. Perhaps this was her chance to explore that passion in a new way, to honor her grandmother's legacy while carving her own path.

With a newfound sense of determination, Charlotte threw herself into her work, organizing shelves and arranging displays with renewed energy. But even as she lost herself in the familiar routines, her mind wandered to **The Velvet Room**, to the possibilities that lay ahead.

She pictured herself on that stage, surrounded by the echoes of her grandmother's presence. She imagined the faces of the crowd, the energy of live music pulsing through the room—the local bands that soured to superstardom. And for a moment, Charlotte allowed herself to dream, to believe that she could be the one to bring the music venue back to life.

As the day wore on and the sun began to set, Charlotte found herself drawn to the old records her grandmother had left her. She picked one up, running her fingers over the worn sleeve, and made a decision. With a deep breath and a fluttering heart, she placed the record on the turntable, ready to take the first step into her new chapter.

The opening notes of a jazzy tune filled the air, and Charlotte closed her eyes, letting the music wash over her. For the first time in a long time, she felt a sense of connection, a thread tying her to the grandmother she had never truly known. And as she swayed to the rhythm, lost in her own thoughts and dreams, Charlotte knew that she was ready to embrace the unexpected, to see where this new path might lead her.

Charlotte's reverie was interrupted by the tinkling of the bell above the bookstore's door. She turned to see Cassie, her vibrant red hair tied back in a messy bun, a look of concern etched on her face.

"Hey, Lottie," Cassie said, her voice soft. "I got your message. Is everything okay?"

Charlotte took a deep breath, trying to find the words to explain the whirlwind of emotions swirling within her. "I... I inherited something from my grandmother."

Cassie's eyes widened. "Your grandmother? I didn't even know you had one."

Charlotte nodded, gesturing for Cassie to follow her to the back of the store. They settled into the worn, comfortable chairs nestled among the shelves, the scent of old books enveloping them.

"She was my dad's mom, I hadn't seen her since I was ten," Charlotte said, her voice barely above a whisper. "She left me a nightclub and music venue, **The Velvet Room**. It was her pride and joy, and now... now it's mine."

Cassie reached out, placing a comforting hand on Charlotte's knee. "Wow, Lottie. That's *huge*. Like you're own **Viper Room**? How are you feeling about all this?"

Charlotte shook her head, a wry smile tugging at her lips. "I don't know, Cass. Part of me is terrified. I mean, what do I know about running a music venue? But another part of me... another part of me is curious. Excited, even."

Cassie squeezed Charlotte's knee, a reassuring gesture. "I get it. It's a lot to take in. But hey, maybe this is the universe's way of giving you a new adventure. A chance to explore a side of yourself you never knew existed."

Charlotte looked up, meeting Cassie's gaze. "You think so?"

"I know so," Cassie said, her tone unwavering. "And I'll be with you every step of the way. Now, let's do some digging and find out more about this Velvet Room of yours."

Together, they huddled over Charlotte's laptop, their faces illuminated by the glow of the screen as they searched for information about **The Velvet Room**. Articles and images filled the screen, painting a picture of a once-thriving music scene, a haven for artists and dreamers alike.

Charlotte's heart raced as she read about the venue's rich history and the legendary performers who had graced its stage. She couldn't help but feel a sense of connection, a pull towards this world that had been her grandmother's passion.

As the night wore on and the research continued, Charlotte found herself dreaming of the possibilities, of the chance to be a part of something bigger than herself. And with Cassie by her side, she felt a flicker of courage, a whisper of hope that maybe, just maybe, she could make her grandmother's legacy her own.

two

. . .

Seattle, Washington

Lottie stood on the sidewalk, gazing up at the old brick building before her. Its walls held the history of a bygone era, built in the early 1920s and still standing tall. Four visible floors rose above her, each with its own purpose and character. The bottom floor was where the music venue resided, an open concept space with a stage that could hold 200 concert guests. Booths and small tables were scattered throughout, providing cozy spots for conversation or drinks from the bar in the back corner. Behind the stage was a mysterious backstage area, off-limits to most but filled with excitement and anticipation for those who were granted access. The second floor housed dressing rooms for performers and a small office for the manager to handle all affairs. Above that, on the third and fourth floors, were apartments where people lived their lives amongst the echoes of music from below.

Lottie's hand trembled as she pushed open the heavy wooden door of the music venue. The hinges groaned, a mournful sound that echoed through the empty space. She stepped inside, her breath catching in her throat.

"Oh," she whispered, her voice barely audible.

The air hung thick with the scent of old wood and forgotten melodies. Lottie's eyes darted around, taking in the familiar yet alien surroundings. Dust motes danced in the thin shafts of light piercing through the grimy windows, like frozen notes suspended in time.

She took another step, the floorboard creaking beneath her weight. The sound startled her, and she instinctively wrapped her arms around herself.

"It's so... quiet," Lottie murmured to herself, her words swallowed by the vastness of the room.

Her gaze fell on the empty stage, its once-vibrant curtains now faded and limp. A lump formed in her throat as she imagined the ghosts of performances past.

The tap of her footsteps echoed as she moved further into the venue. Each step stirred up more dust, more memories. The musty smell of age and neglect filled her nostrils, making her eyes water.

"What am I supposed to do with you?" Lottie asked the empty room, her voice trembling. The silence that answered her was deafening.

She ran her fingers along the bar, leaving trails in the dust. The wood felt warm beneath her touch, as if it held onto the heat of countless nights filled with music and laughter.

Lottie closed her eyes, overwhelmed by the weight of her inheritance. "I don't know if I'm ready for this, Evelyn," she whispered, her words a prayer to the spirits of the venue.

Lottie's eyes fluttered open, catching sight of the old jukebox in the corner. A memory washed over her, vivid and bittersweet.

"I remember you," she said softly, approaching the machine. Her fingers traced the chrome edges, leaving smudges in the dust. "Gramma used to lift me up so I could pick a song."

She chuckled quietly, the sound echoing in the empty space. "I always chose **'Purple Rain'**. Every single time."

Lottie's gaze drifted to the stage again. She walked towards it, her footsteps slow and measured. As she climbed the three rickety steps, she could almost hear the phantom cheers of an imaginary audience.

Standing center stage, Lottie spread her arms wide, picturing the venue in its glory days. "This could be something again," she mused aloud, her voice gaining strength. "Maybe... maybe I could make it something."

She turned, facing the backstage area. The tattered velvet curtains parted easily under her touch, revealing a maze of old equipment and discarded instruments.

"Oh wow," Lotte breathed, picking up a dusty guitar. "I bet you've got some stories to tell."

As she explored further, ideas began to form in her mind. "We could set up a green room here," she muttered, gesturing to a small alcove. "And over there... that could be perfect for sound equipment."

Returning to the main area, Lottie's eyes fell on the bar. She ran her hand along its surface, picturing it polished and gleaming. "A little TLC and you'd be serving drinks in no time," she told it, a small smile playing on her lips.

For the first time since entering, Lottie felt a spark of excitement. "Maybe this isn't so impossible after all," she said to herself, her voice echoing with newfound determination in the empty venue.

But as quickly as the excitement had come, it vanished, replaced by a crushing wave of doubt. Lottie's shoulders slumped, her breath catching in her throat.

"Who am I kidding?" she whispered, her voice trembling. "I don't know the first thing about running a music venue."

She sank onto a nearby stool, her head in her hands. The weight of responsibility pressed down on her like a physical force.

"What if I mess this up?" Lottie's thoughts raced. "What if I can't live up to Gramma Evie's legacy?"

Her eyes darted around the room, suddenly seeing not potential, but problems. Peeling paint, outdated wiring, years of neglect. It was overwhelming.

"I'm just... me," she said softly, her voice barely audible. "How can I possibly handle all of this?"

As if in response, a floorboard creaked beneath her feet. Lottie looked down, noticing a slight protrusion. Curious, she knelt and pried at the loose board.

"What's this?" she muttered, pulling out a dusty cardboard box.

Inside, she found a treasure trove of old photographs and papers. Her hands trembled as she lifted out a faded picture of a young woman with familiar eyes, standing proudly in front of the venue.

"Gramma Evie?" Lottie gasped, studying the image. "You look so... alive."

She rifled through more photos, each one revealing a different facet of her grandmother's life. Evie with famous musicians, Evie behind the bar, Evie on stage.

"I had no idea," Lottie whispered, her curiosity piqued. "Who were you really, Gramma?"

Lottie's fingers traced the edges of the photographs, her mind whirling with possibilities. She stood up, clutching the box to her chest, and looked around the venue with fresh eyes.

"Maybe..." she murmured, her voice gaining strength. "Maybe I can do this."

She set the box down on the bar and pulled out a faded concert flyer. The paper crackled beneath her touch, like the whisper of a long-forgotten melody.

"Gramma built this place from nothing," Lottie thought, her resolve solidifying. "She created something beautiful here. Something that mattered."

With a deep breath, she squared her shoulders and strode to the center of the room. The floorboards creaked beneath her feet, a familiar sound that now felt like an encouragement.

"Alright, Gramma," she said aloud, her voice echoing in the empty space. "I hear you. I'll do it. I'll bring this place back to life."

Lottie's heart raced with a mix of fear and excitement. She glanced at the stage, imagining it filled with musicians, the air electric with sound.

"It won't be easy," she admitted to herself. "But nothing worth doing ever is, right?"

She walked to the front door, her steps more confident now. As she reached for the handle, she paused, looking back at the venue—*her* venue now.

"This is it," Lottie whispered, a small smile playing on her lips. "A new chapter. For me, for this place, for music."

With that, she stepped out into the sunlight, ready to face whatever challenges lay ahead. The door closed behind her with a soft click, like the final note of a song - an ending, but also a beginning.

three

. . .

A Month Later

The dust danced in the sunbeams as Lottie pushed open the heavy door to **The Velvet Room**. It had been a month since the papers were signed, a month since this treasure trove of melodies and memories had become hers. She ran her fingers over the worn counter, heart thrumming like the opening riff to an old favorite song. This was more than business; it was a sacred promise to keep her grandmother's spirit alive within these walls.

She envisioned the space transformed - vibrant and pulsing with life, each corner echoing with lyrical whispers of the past and the electric anticipation of the present. The stage would be a beacon, a place where both weathered vinyl and fresh voices would spin tales under the spell of soft lights. It wouldn't just be a venue; it would be a sanctuary for souls stitched together by chords and choruses.

Lottie carefully navigated her way through the cluttered backstage area, her eyes scanning over peeling posters and forgotten guitar picks scattered across the floor. As she stepped onto a staircase leading up to the dressing rooms and manager's office, the walls creaked beneath her weight, causing her to freeze in place. Her mind raced with thoughts of what could be making such a noise.

Sensing movement from above, Lottie strained her ears to listen. The sound of footsteps echoed through the halls, growing louder as they approached from the upper two levels. Curiosity overtaking her, she made her way towards the staircase that led to the upper levels.

As she climbed the stairs, Lottie was hit with a strong scent of cologne and cigarette smoke coming from one of the rooms. She cautiously crept closer, trying to remain undetected. Through a slightly open door, she could see a television playing in the room and hear voices coming from within.

Realizing that someone was living in this abandoned building, Lottie knocked on their door. When there was no answer, she knocked harder, almost pounding on the door. After several moments with no response, she pushed open the door.

Her breath caught in her throat at the sight before her. Standing in front of her was a man who exuded charisma and sex appeal. With long dirty blonde hair, piercing green eyes, and sun-kissed skin, he looked preserved for his age. Dressed effortlessly in worn jeans and a simple white t-shirt, he seemed completely at ease in his surroundings.

"Hi," Lottie said nervously, waving her hand. "Who are you? And why do you live here?"

The man leaned against his open door with a relaxed posture. "And who are you?" he countered.

Lottie felt his gaze travel down her body, scrutinizing her with his intense stare. "My name's Charlotte, and I own this place," she stated confidently. "And, who are you again?"

He ran a hand through his hair before resting it in his jeans pocket. "Alex," he softly replied, without a hint of a smile. "And you own this place? Where's Evie?"

Charlotte's heart sank at the mention of her grandmother. "Evelyn is—*was* my grandmother," she corrected herself. "She passed away recently, and I inherited the building."

A small smile played on Alex's lips. "You must be Lottie," he said knowingly.

Feeling bold, Charlotte began to explore the living area that she had unintentionally barged into. Everywhere she looked, there were rugs, tapestries, vases, and beads adorning every surface. *A Bohemian nightmare…*Gold records hung on the walls, along with posters of a familiar rock band.

As she made her way towards one of the posters, Charlotte couldn't help but feel a sense of nostalgia wash over her. It was a poster for the Grammy Award-winning rock group, **"Hollow Reign"**. Her best friend's older brother had **Hollow Reign** plastered all over his walls when she was growing up.

But what caught her attention even more were the multiple posters of the same band scattered throughout the room. Her eyes widened as she slowly turned to face the man across from her, his arms crossed against his chest and his feet casually crossed at his ankles.

"Are you Alex King?" she asked in disbelief.

With a slow nod of his head, he confirmed her suspicions. Alex King—the reclusive rock legend who seemed almost mythical in person. Surrounded by boxes of faded lyrics and tarnished trophies, he radiated an aura of mystery and intrigue. Shadows clung to him like adoring fans to a star, but he shone through like a constellation of his own creation.

"Didn't expect company," his voice rumbled, a low melody that resonated within the cramped space.

"Neither did I," Lottie replied, her words cautious yet laced with the thrill of discovery.

"Why here?" she asked, unable to mask the intrigue lacing her tone.

"Sanctuary," was all he said, his gaze returning to a cracked vinyl in his hands. The air between them thickened with stories untold, his presence an enigma wrapped in denim and disillusionment. He was living history, a breathing anthology of a thousand songs, tucked away in the apartment floors of **The Velvet Room**.

"Did my grandmother know you lived here?" Lottie asked, curious.

Alex let go a small laugh, "Of course, she's the one who gave me an open-ended lease."

Lottie raised an eyebrow. Her gaze caught on his rugged features; the salt-and-pepper strands that fell loosely over his brow, the way his eyes – sharp and blue as a winter sky – hinted at storms weathered and battles fought. His presence was like a chord struck deep in her chest, resonant and unexpected.

"Still," she began, tucking a strand of black hair behind her ear, "I didn't expect... Well, someone like you to be here."

"Someone like me?" Alex arched an eyebrow, a ghost of a smile playing on his lips.

"Someone who..." Lottie's words trailed off as she grappled with the juxtaposition of her shy nature against the pull of his enigmatic aura. "...has stories to tell."

"Ah." Alex leaned back against a stack of forgotten records, the slight creak of aged vinyl beneath him. "And what makes you think I've got stories?"

"Doesn't everyone?" Lottie countered, her curiosity piquing despite her reservations. She noticed the subtle shift in his stance, a wall coming down brick by brick.

"True," he conceded, the lines around his eyes softening. "But some are better left unsung."

There was a moment then, a silent understanding that fluttered between them like a melody only they could hear. Lottie's pulse quickened, her cheeks warming under the weight of his gaze. She wanted to delve deeper, to unearth the lyrics of his past and compose them into the future of **The Velvet Room**.

"Perhaps," she said, her voice steadier now, "but sometimes the unsung ones resonate the most."

Alex regarded her with a mix of surprise and something akin to admiration. Lottie could almost see the walls he'd built around himself trembling, the bricks loosening under the influence of her gentle persistence.

"Maybe you're right," he admitted, and for a fleeting second, his guard slipped, revealing a glint of vulnerability.

Lottie's heart skipped as she watched him, this man who had lived a thousand lives in the span of a few decades. The urge to reach out, to close the distance between them, was almost overwhelming. But she hesitated, her innate caution grappling with the raw attraction that simmered just below the surface.

"Maybe I am," she whispered, more to herself than to him, as she retreated down the steps, leaving Alex King – the man, the myth, the music – veiled once more in the twilight of **The Velvet Room.**

four

. . .

ottie brushed a strand of black hair from her forehead, leaving a smudge of white paint in its wake. The walls of **The Velvet Room** hummed with the promise of new life under her diligent hands. She moved methodically along the once-dingy interior, now blossoming with fresh vibrancy beneath each stroke.

Alex's presence lingered in the periphery of her senses, an unobtrusive shadow that drifted within the apartment above. Their coexistence within the venue had become a dance of silent acknowledgment—a nod here, a half-smile there, both skirting the edge of something neither fully understood.

She caught glimpses of him sometimes—his weathered jeans frayed at the edges, his long hair tied back revealing the storied lines of his face. He'd appear like a wraith at the top of the stairs, watching her with those piercing blue eyes that seemed to strip away the years and see right into the marrow of the place.

Today, Lottie noticed Alex leaning against the railing, a guitar cradled in his arms as if it were part of him. His fingers danced across the strings, coaxing out a melody so poignant it made her heart ache. The notes floated down, settling around her like an unseen caress.

"Sounds beautiful," she called up, her voice cutting through the quiet with the delicacy of a feather.

"Old habits," he replied, his tone a mixture of nostalgia and something darker she couldn't place.

Lottie dipped her roller back into the paint tray and resumed her work, but her attention remained tethered to the man above. Alex King was a puzzle wrapped in an enigma—an aged poster of a rock god who had burned too bright and faded into obscurity.

As she painted, Lottie found herself stealing glances at his solitary figure. He moved with a grace that belied his rugged exterior, every gesture a testament to a life lived at full volume now muted. There was wisdom etched in the crow's feet at the corners of his eyes, and sorrow in the set of his jaw—a silent symphony of experience that drew her in.

"Ever miss it?" she asked on impulse during one of his brief descents to the main floor for water.

"Miss what?" His reply came slow, cautious.

"The stage. The roar of the crowd."

"Sometimes," he admitted after a pause, his gaze drifting past her to the empty stage. "But the quiet has its own music, you know?"

Lottie nodded, even though the quiet had never roared for her as it must have for him. And yet, she thought she understood—the peace of being heard without clamor, of finding harmony in silence.

"Guess we're both renovating more than just this old place," she mused aloud, not really expecting a response.

Alex's lips curled into a knowing smirk before he retreated back to his refuge. Lottie watched him go, her pulse quickening in time with the hammering of nails and the rhythm of her own breath.

Lottie swept her brush along the wall, the bristles whispering secrets into the curves of old plaster. Golden afternoon sun spilled through the windows, casting a warm glow on the dust motes that danced like tiny fairies in the air.

"Careful with those," Alex's voice rumbled from behind a stack of amplifiers, disrupting the quiet ballet of light and dust. He emerged holding a box of faded photographs and frayed concert tickets, his blue eyes tinged with nostalgia.

"Memories?" Lottie's voice was gentle, her question hanging delicately between them.

"Echoes," he corrected, setting the box down with a reverence reserved for sacred relics. "Reminders of a different era."

"May I?" She gestured toward the box, her movements tentative, as if requesting permission to enter a secret chamber of his soul.

Alex hesitated, a battle flickering across his features before he nodded. "Just be careful. They're... fragile."

She thumbed through the photos, each one a window into a world of bright lights and ecstatic faces. Alex, with his mane wild and untamed, commanded stages that now lived only in these frozen moments. She felt the weight of his history, the gravity of countless eyes that had witnessed his rise and fall.

"Looks like you were adored," she remarked, her voice soft but laced with an edge of awe.

"Adoration is fleeting," he said, the words heavy with truth. "It fades faster than the last note of a closing song."

Lottie paused, sensing the rawness in his voice. She met his gaze, finding the vulnerability he so rarely allowed to surface. It was like catching a chord struck in minor key, resonant and full of unspoken sorrow.

"Is that why you stopped? The fading?"

"Partly." He sighed, running a hand through his hair. The action dislodged a memory, sending it tumbling to the forefront. "Music was everything. Then one day, it just wasn't enough. The applause couldn't drown out the emptiness."

"Emptiness?" Her curiosity piqued, bridging the gap between them with genuine concern.

"Have you ever loved something so much it consumes you?" he asked, his eyes searching hers. "Until there's nothing left but the shell of who you once were?"

"Maybe not to that extent," Lottie admitted, "but music... it's a part of me. It's like breathing."

"Exactly," he murmured, a ghost of a smile touching his lips. "But imagine if every breath was judged, critiqued, sold to the highest bidder. Would you still cherish each inhale and exhale?"

"Probably not," she conceded, her fingers tracing the edge of a ticket stub. "So, what's your favorite song? The one that still feels like a fresh breath?"

"Ah," he chuckled, the sound soft and unexpected. "A song by this obscure band from the '70s, *Nights in Silver Satin.*' Not many know it, but it's got this riff that feels like... coming home."

"Mine's *Whispers of the Wind,*" Lottie shared, smiling at the coincidence. "An indie track my mom used to play. It speaks of love like a quiet revolution, stirring beneath the surface."

"Sounds beautiful," Alex said, leaning closer. Their shared confessions wove a thread of connection, pulling them into a tapestry of melodies and lyrics. They spoke of rhythms and rhymes, dissecting harmonies and crescendos until the music venue around them faded into a backdrop for their symphony of words.

As the sun dipped below the horizon, shadows played upon the walls, and their conversation lingered in the hushed tones of dusk. In the silence that followed, a new understanding passed between them—a mutual recognition of souls entwined by the love of a language that spoke without needing to make a sound.

* * *

LOTTIE LEANED against the freshly painted wall, a soft sigh escaping her lips as she watched the dust motes dance in the slanting light. The room, once cluttered with memories and echoes of raucous nights, now held the promise of new beginnings. Her fingers curled around the handle of a paintbrush, the bristles stiff with drying cerulean blue—a bold choice for the venue that mirrored the boldness of her decision to take this leap.

"Never thought I'd find myself here," she murmured, her voice barely louder than the whisper of fabric as she wiped a smudge of paint from her cheek. Lottie's life had been a neatly organized playlist, each day a familiar track played on repeat. But inheriting **The Velvet Room** had scratched the record, sending the needle skidding into uncharted grooves.

She glanced toward the apartment hatch, half-expecting to see Alex emerge like some reclusive phantom. His presence in her grandmother's venue was an enigma wrapped in a riddle, punctuated by those piercing blue eyes that seemed to strip away her layers of reserve. And yet, despite the disarray he brought to her orderly world, there was an undeniable allure in the chaos—a siren call to the part of her that craved a melody less predictable.

The silence stretched on, filled only with the hum of anticipation. Lottie's mind wandered to the challenges ahead, the inevitable clash of her structured calm against Alex's stormy past. Could **The Velvet Room** withstand the discord of their mingling lives, or would it amplify the fears that whispered doubts in the back of her mind?

"Renovations going well?" Alex's voice cut through her reverie, deep and resonant like the bass line of a long-forgotten ballad.

"Better than expected," she replied, her heart skipping a beat as she turned to face him. The setting sun framed his silhouette, casting a golden glow that softened the edges of his rugged features.

"Good." He nodded, the corners of his mouth hinting at a smile that never quite reached his eyes. "Just remember, Lottie, buildings aren't the only things in need of repair."

His words hung in the air—a poignant note in the symphony of unsaid thoughts between them. She wanted to delve deeper, to explore the harmony they could create together, but fear held her back. Lottie knew all too well that the most enthralling music often sprung from the deepest pain.

"Alex—" she started, but the look in his eyes stopped her. There was a storm brewing behind those clear blues, a tempest of history and heartache that promised to test the limits of their newfound connection.

"Let's just focus on the venue for now," he said curtly, turning away to conceal whatever emotions threatened to spill over.

Lottie watched him retreat into the shadows, her pulse racing with a mix of desire and dread. The chapter closed with the echo of their unfinished conversation, leaving questions suspended like notes in a song awaiting resolution. What lay ahead for Lottie and Alex was as uncertain as the flickering lights of **The Velvet Room**—a duet of passion and regret playing out beneath the surface of their everyday interactions.

Lottie continued her renovation, hands moving rhythmically, stripping away the old wallpaper as if she were peeling back the years that had settled into the very walls of **The Velvet Room.** Dust motes danced in the slanting beams of sunlight that fought their way through the partially covered windows, reflecting her determination in each glittering speck. The scent of aged adhesive mingled with the mustiness of antiquated wood, a pungent reminder of the venue's storied past.

She paused, allowing herself a moment to soak in the sounds that filled the room—an orchestra of renovation. The clink of tools echoed off bare walls, punctuated by the occasional creak of floorboards underfoot, speaking to the history they supported. In the background, the soft hum of a radio played a classic rock tune, a haunting melody that seemed almost in conversation with the ghosts of musical legends past.

Lottie ran her fingers along the grooves in the wood paneling, tracing the notes of memories imprinted there. She could almost hear the echoes of cheering crowds, the vibrations of bass lines that once set the air on fire. Now, there was only the quiet anticipation of rebirth, the space eagerly awaiting the new harmonies and lyrics it would soon cradle.

Her breath caught as she envisioned the future—a cacophony of live performances, the air thick with the electricity of amplified guitars, and the warmth of shared experiences. Once a haven for so many, **The Velvet Room** would pulse with life again, its heart beating in time with the music it housed.

And somewhere in that dreamt-up symphony, the image of Alex lingered—a shadowy figure with eyes like clear winter skies, carrying a tune of mystery and sorrow. Lottie's own heart kept tempo with an unfamiliar rhythm, one that spoke of possibilities wrapped in caution tape—of bridges yet to be crossed and songs yet to be sung.

five

. . .

$\mathcal{P}$aint fumes filled Lottie's nostrils as she dragged the roller brush across the faded wall, each stroke a promise to breathe new life into the music venue. Flecks of robin's egg blue speckled her cheek, a mark of her determination. She stepped back, surveying her progress, the freshly painted surface a testament to her commitment.

From the shadows of the balcony, Alex watched her, his eyes tracing the delicate curve of her neck, the way her black hair cascaded over her shoulders as she worked. He leaned against the railing, his fingers absentmindedly strumming an invisible guitar, a habit he couldn't shake. There was something about her, an aura of gentleness mixed with quiet strength, that intrigued him.

Lottie moved to the stage, her fingertips grazing the worn wood, feeling the echoes of countless performances. She knelt down, examining the loose boards, her mind already piecing together a plan to restore its former glory. As she worked, she hummed a melody, a soft tune that drifted through the empty venue like a ghost of its musical past.

Alex's ears perked up at the sound of her voice, a shiver running down his spine. It had been so long since music had stirred something within him, the jaded cynicism of the industry having taken its toll. But here, in this moment, watching Lottie pour her heart into the place, he felt a flicker of something he thought he'd lost - inspiration.

Lottie stood up, brushing the dust from her vintage jeans, unaware of the pair of piercing blue eyes that followed her every move. She turned, her gaze landing on the stage lights, their bulbs coated in a layer of neglect. A soft sigh escaped her lips as she envisioned the transformation, the way the lights would shine down on the stage once more, illuminating the raw talent that would grace its presence.

Lottie hadn't seen Alex that morning and wondered if he was okay. She decided to go and pay him a visit.

Once inside, the apartment seemed to shrink around them as they delved deeper into their shared passion, the outside world fading away until only the two of them remained. Lottie found herself leaning closer to Alex, drawn in by the intensity of his gaze and the warmth of his voice. She couldn't help but notice the way his hands moved as he spoke, as if conducting an invisible orchestra.

"You know, there's something about a well-crafted lyric that just gets me every time," Alex confessed, his eyes sparkling with enthusiasm. "The way the words can paint a picture, evoke an emotion, tell a story..."

Lottie's gaze lingered on Alex's rugged features, taking in the way the soft light from the apartment window played across his face. There was a vulnerability in his eyes that she hadn't noticed before, a glimpse of the man beneath the mystery.

"You know," Alex said, his voice low and contemplative, "being in the music industry isn't all it's cracked up to be." He ran a hand through his salt-and-pepper hair, his eyes distant. "The fame, the fortune... it comes at a price."

Lottie leaned forward, her curiosity piqued. "What do you mean?"

Alex sighed, his shoulders slumping slightly. "When you're in the spotlight, everyone wants a piece of you. Your music, your image, your soul..." He shook his head. "It's easy to lose yourself in the chaos."

Lottie's heart ached for him, for the pain she could see etched into the lines of his face. She reached out instinctively, her hand coming to rest on his arm. "I can't imagine what that must have been like," she said softly.

Alex's gaze met hers, and for a moment, the air between them crackled with electricity. She could feel the heat of his skin beneath her fingertips, the steady thrum of his pulse. "It's not a life I would wish on anyone," he said, his voice barely above a whisper.

Lottie swallowed hard, her mouth suddenly dry. She knew she should pull away, put some distance between them, but she couldn't seem to make herself move. The attraction she felt for him was like a physical force, drawing her in like a moth to a flame.

Alex's eyes darkened, and Lottie wondered if he could sense the effect he was having on her. His gaze dropped to her lips, and for a heart-stopping moment, she thought he might kiss her. But then he blinked, and the spell was broken.

"I should go," she said, her voice rough. "Get back to work."

Alex nodded, his heart racing. "Yeah, of course."

She stood up, brushing off her jeans. "Thanks for the talk, Alex. It was...nice."

Alex smiled, a genuine smile that lit up his whole face. "Yeah, it was." He hesitated for a moment, then reached out and tucked a strand of hair behind her ear. "See ya around."

LOTTIE DESCENDED THE STAIRS, her fingers trailing along the worn wooden banister. The creak of the old steps echoed in the empty venue, a reminder of the work that lay ahead. But her mind was elsewhere, still lost in the memory of Alex's low, rumbling laughter and the way his eyes had sparkled with shared understanding.

She wandered through the venue, her gaze roaming over the faded posters and dusty instruments. Everywhere she looked, she saw traces of Alex - a guitar pick wedged between the floorboards, a scribbled note taped to the soundboard. It was as if he had become part of the very fabric of the place.

Lottie's heart raced as she pictured him moving through the space, his lean body graceful and assured. She imagined his fingers, rough with calluses, brushing against her skin, igniting sparks of desire.

She shook her head, trying to clear the dangerous thoughts. *This was madness.* Alex was nearly twice her age, a world-weary musician with a lifetime of experiences she could hardly fathom. *What could he possibly see in a naive, sheltered girl like her?*

And yet... the way he looked at her, the intensity in his gaze, the tenderness in his touch... it made her feel seen, understood in a way she never had before. As if he could peer straight into her soul and find beauty in all the broken pieces.

Lottie sank onto the edge of the stage, her legs dangling over the side. She closed her eyes, letting the silence wash over her. In her mind, she could hear the first strains of a melody taking shape, the notes weaving together in a haunting refrain of longing and possibility.

When she opened her eyes again, she knew with sudden certainty that everything had changed. The connection between her and Alex was more than just friendship, more than just shared passion for music. It was a force of nature, wild and uncontrollable, threatening to sweep her away.

Lottie took a deep, shuddering breath. She was standing on the edge of a precipice, poised between the safety of solitude and the exhilarating danger of the unknown.

One step forward, and she would be falling, tumbling headlong into an uncertain future. One step back, and she would be forever wondering what might have been.

In that suspended moment, the whole world seemed to hold its breath, waiting for her choice.

six

. . .

The faint scent of fresh paint mingled with sawdust, tickling Lottie's nose as she settled into the rickety chair. Across the small table, Alex's piercing blue eyes met hers, igniting a flutter in her chest.

"So, what kind of music speaks to your soul?" Alex's deep voice rumbled, a hint of curiosity peeking through his guarded exterior.

Lottie tucked a strand of black hair behind her ear, her mind racing. She didn't expect to see him so soon—but was glad to see he hadn't waited. "I've always been drawn to the classics. The raw emotion of Janis Joplin, the poetry of Bob Dylan..." She trailed off, suddenly self-conscious. *Would he think her tastes old-fashioned?*

But Alex's face lit up. "Ah, a woman after my own heart. Nothing beats the authenticity of those legends."

As they delved deeper into their musical preferences, Lottie found herself gesticulating more animatedly, her usual shyness melting away. The construction noise faded into the background, replaced by the invisible notes of their shared passion.

"What about you?" Lotte asked, leaning forward. "Any guilty pleasures in your playlist?"

Alex chuckled, the sound warm and rich. "Let's just say I have a soft spot for 80s power ballads. But if you tell anyone, I'll deny it."

Lottie laughed, a genuine, full-bodied sound that surprised her. *When was the last time she'd felt this comfortable with someone?*

As their laughter subsided, Lottie's gaze drifted around the venue. In her mind's eye, she could see it transformed - fairy lights twinkling, the air thick with anticipation, the stage alive with raw talent.

"You know," she began, her voice soft but filled with conviction, "I have this vision for this place. I want to create a haven for music lovers, where artists can bare their souls and audiences can feel every note."

Alex leaned in, his eyes never leaving her face. Lottie's heart raced, but she pressed on, her passion overwhelming her usual reticence.

"Imagine intimate acoustic sets, where you can hear a pin drop during the quiet moments. Or raucous punk shows where the energy is so electric, you can almost see it crackling in the air."

As she spoke, Lottie's hands moved of their own accord, painting pictures in the air. She described her dreams of fostering connections, of creating magical moments that would linger in people's memories long after the last chord faded.

Throughout it all, Alex listened intently, his expression unreadable. Lottie wondered what he was thinking. Did he find her naive? Overly idealistic?

But as she finished speaking, a small smile played at the corners of his mouth. "You've got quite the vision there, Charlotte," he said, using her full name for the first time. The way it rolled off his tongue sent a shiver down her spine.

Lottie blushed, suddenly aware of how carried away she'd gotten. "Is it too much?" she asked, her insecurity creeping back in.

Alex shook his head, his eyes twinkling. "Not at all. In fact, I think you might be onto something special here." Alex leaned forward, his elbows resting on the small table. "Tell me more about these intimate performances you envision. How do you plan to create that connection between artist and audience?"

Lottie's heart raced. She hadn't expected him to be so interested. "Well," she began, her voice soft but growing more confident, "I want to create an atmosphere where every person feels like they're part of something special. Maybe we could have some shows where the audience sits in a circle around the performer, or..."

As she spoke, Alex's eyes never left her face. His initial skepticism had melted away, replaced by genuine curiosity. He nodded, encouraging her to continue.

"What about the impact?" he asked, his deep voice sending a shiver down her spine. "How do you see this changing people's lives?"

Lottie paused, considering. "Music has the power to heal, to inspire. I want this place to be a sanctuary where people can come to feel less alone."

Something shifted in Alex's expression. His eyes grew distant, as if seeing something beyond the dusty walls of the venue. "I remember that feeling," he murmured, almost to himself. "The rush of connecting with a crowd, the way a song can make the whole world disappear."

Lottie held her breath, sensing she was witnessing something rare and precious. Alex's guard had dropped, revealing a glimpse of the passionate musician he once was.

A spark of inspiration ignited in his eyes. "You know," he said, a hint of excitement creeping into his voice, "maybe there's still some magic left in this old place after all."

The air crackled with creative energy as Lottie and Alex huddled closer, their voices rising and falling in an excited rhythm. Lottie's hands moved animatedly, punctuating her words as she spoke.

"What if we did themed nights?" she suggested, her brown eyes wide with excitement. "Like, 'Throwback Thursdays' for classic rock, or 'Fusion Fridays' where we blend different genres?"

Alex nodded, his salt-and-pepper hair catching the dim light. "I like that. We could even do 'Unsigned Sundays' to give local talent a platform."

Lottie felt a thrill run through her. This was it - the spark she'd been waiting for. "Oh! And what about intimate acoustic sets? We could create a cozy corner with fairy lights and cushions."

"Now you're talking," Alex said, his deep voice tinged with enthusiasm. "I can almost see it - the soft glow, the hushed audience, the raw emotion in the music."

As they bounced ideas back and forth, Lottie couldn't help but marvel at how easily they connected. Here she was, shy, bookish Lottie, planning a music revolution with a rock legend. Life had a funny way of surprising you.

Lottie leaned forward, her vintage-inspired blouse rustling softly. "What's the most memorable performance you've ever seen?" she asked, her voice barely above a whisper.

Alex's piercing blue eyes grew distant, lost in memory. "It was a Nirvana show, '91. The energy was... electric. Raw. Cobain had this way of making you feel like he was singing just for you, you know?"

Lottie nodded, enraptured. She could almost hear the distorted guitars, feel the press of the crowd.

"What about you?" Alex asked, his gaze refocusing on her.

Lottie bit her lip, thinking. "It was actually a small coffeehouse gig. This unknown singer-songwriter, her voice like honey and smoke. She sang about heartbreak and hope, and I swear, everyone in that room was crying by the end."

Alex smiled, a genuine warmth spreading across his rugged features. "That's the magic, isn't it? When the music transcends everything else."

They fell into a comfortable silence, the weight of shared understanding settling between them. Lottie's mind raced with possibilities, with the potential of what they could create together.

After a moment, Alex spoke again, his voice low and thoughtful. "You know, Lottie, I think we might be onto something here. Something... real."

Lottie's heart skipped a beat. She reached out, her fingers trembling slightly as they made contact with Alex's weathered hand. The touch was electric, a silent affirmation of their shared dreams and the unexpected bond they had formed.

Alex's eyes met hers, a knowing smile playing at the corners of his mouth. In that moment, Lottie saw more than just the former rock star - she saw a kindred spirit, someone who understood the transformative power of music as deeply as she did.

"I think you're right," Lottie murmured, her voice barely audible over the faint hum of construction in the background. "This could be something... extraordinary."

Alex's fingers intertwined with hers, his touch surprisingly gentle. "It's been a long time since I've felt this excited about music," he admitted, a hint of vulnerability in his deep voice.

Lottie's mind raced with visions of what they could create together. The intimate performances, the connection between artist and audience, the magic that could unfold within these walls. It was all within reach now.

"So," Alex said, his blue eyes twinkling with a mixture of mischief and determination, "where do we start?"

Lottie grinned, feeling a surge of confidence she hadn't experienced in years. "We start by dreaming big," she replied, "and then we make those dreams a reality."

As they began to discuss their plans, the air around them seemed to crackle with possibility. Lottie knew that this was just the beginning of an incredible journey - one that would change not only the venue but their lives as well.

seven

. . .

The flickering candlelight danced across Lottie's face, reflecting in her warm brown eyes as she gazed at Alex across the intimate table. Shadows shifted and swayed on the café walls, cocooning them in their own private world.

Alex sat stiffly, jaw clenched, his brooding blue eyes guarded beneath a furrowed brow. Even now, vestiges of his rock star persona clung to him like a well-worn leather jacket. But Lottie sensed the vulnerability simmering beneath the surface, saw the weariness etched in the lines around his mouth.

Slowly, hesitantly, she reached out a delicate hand. Her fingertips brushed his rough knuckles. "Alex," she murmured, her voice soft as a sigh. "Talk to me."

He glanced up, startled by her touch. Lottie's breath caught at the intensity in his ice-blue gaze, at the desire and anguish warring there. She wondered fleetingly if casual sex would be easier than this. Fewer complications. No messy feelings.

But no. She wanted more. Wanted him - all of him, scars and baggage included. Her thumb traced soothing circles on his skin, silently imploring him to let her in.

Alex swallowed hard. "I'm not sure where to start, Lottie," he rasped, voice roughened by whiskey and regret. "I've made so many mistakes. Seen and done things I'm not proud of."

"It's okay," she breathed. "I'm here. I'm listening."

The air crackled with tension, with unspoken promises. Lottie's heart thudded against her ribs. This was it. The moment everything could change between them.

Under the table, Alex turned his hand to lace his fingers through hers. Gripping tight. Holding on as if she were his only lifeline in a turbulent sea of memories.

He took a shuddering breath. And started to speak.

His gaze remained fixed on their intertwined hands as the words spilled from his lips, a torrent of pain and regret. "Fame... it's not what people think. It's a constant pressure, always being watched, judged." Alex's voice was low, raw with emotion. "The expectations, the demands... it eats away at you."

Lottie leaned in, her free hand coming to rest on his forearm. A silent gesture of support, of understanding. She could feel the tension thrumming through his body, the weight of his past bearing down on him.

"I turned to alcohol, drugs... anything to numb the pain, to escape the reality of my life." His confession hung heavy in the air between them. "It was a downward spiral. I lost myself, Lottie. Lost sight of what mattered."

Lottie's heart ached for him, for the lost and broken man beneath the rock star facade. She squeezed his hand, her thumb brushing over his knuckles. "But you found your way back," she murmured. "You're here now, Alex. That's what counts."

He laughed, a harsh, bitter sound. "Am I? Sometimes I wonder if I ever really left that life behind. If I'll ever be free of it."

"You will," Lottie said fiercely. "I know you will. You're stronger than you think, Alex. You've already come so far."

His eyes met hers then, searching, probing. Looking for the truth behind her words. Lottie held his gaze, willing him to see the faith she had in him, the belief that he could overcome anything.

Memories flickered through Alex's mind like the flashing bulbs of paparazzi cameras. The roar of the crowd, the thrill of the stage lights, the rush of adrenaline as he poured his heart out into the microphone. But behind the scenes, the cracks had begun to show. Late nights turned into early mornings, fueled by a toxic cocktail of alcohol and pills. He'd sought solace in the bottom of a bottle, in the arms of faceless groupies, in anything that could dull the ache in his chest.

"I was drowning," he murmured, his gaze distant, lost in the past. "Suffocating under the weight of it all. The expectations, the pressure, the constant scrutiny. I couldn't breathe, couldn't think. So I numbed myself however I could, just to make it through another day."

Lottie's heart clenched, her eyes stinging with unshed tears. She couldn't begin to imagine the toll it had taken on him, the scars he carried beneath the surface. But she saw them now, raw and exposed, and her admiration for him only grew.

"You're so brave," she whispered, her voice thick with emotion. "To have gone through all of that and come out the other side. To be sitting here now, sharing your story with me. That takes incredible strength, Alex."

He shook his head, a rueful smile tugging at the corner of his mouth. "I don't feel strong," he admitted. "Most days, I feel like I'm barely holding it together. Like I'm one wrong move away from slipping back into old habits, old patterns."

"But you haven't," Lottie pointed out gently. "You're here, in this moment, choosing to be better. Choosing to heal. That's the bravest thing you can do."

Alex's eyes met hers, and for a moment, the rest of the world fell away. In the soft glow of the candlelight, Lottie saw a flicker of something in his gaze - gratitude, perhaps, or a tentative hope. A sense that maybe, just maybe, he could find his way out of the darkness and into the light.

As Alex continued to share the painful memories of his past, Lottie found herself reaching across the table, her hand seeking his. Her fingers brushed against his knuckles, a feather-light touch that seemed to hold the weight of unspoken understanding. She felt his hand tremble slightly beneath hers, and she gave a gentle squeeze, a silent promise that she was there, that he wasn't alone.

The café around them seemed to fade into the background, the gentle hum of conversation and the clink of cups and saucers becoming distant and muffled. In that moment, it was as if they were the only two people in the world, cocooned in a bubble of intimacy that was both fragile and precious.

Lottie's thumb traced small circles on the back of Alex's hand, a soothing rhythm that seemed to anchor him as he spoke. She watched as the tension in his shoulders slowly eased, as the lines of his face softened, and she realized that this was a side of him that few people ever saw. The vulnerable, unguarded Alex, stripped bare of his rock star persona and the walls he'd built around himself.

"I never thought I'd find someone who could understand," Alex murmured, his voice raw with emotion. "Someone who could see past the mistakes I've made, the person I used to be."

As Alex's story came to an end, a heavy silence settled over them, the weight of his words lingering in the air like a tangible presence. Lottie's hand remained on his, her thumb absently tracing circles on his skin as she processed all that he'd shared. She could feel the rough calluses on his fingers, a testament to the countless hours he'd spent pouring his heart and soul into his music.

In the flickering candlelight, Alex's face was a study in contrasts - the lines of pain and weariness etched into his skin, but also the glimmer of hope and vulnerability in his eyes. It was a face that Lottie had come to know so well, but in that moment, it felt like she was seeing him for the first time - not as the rock legend or the reclusive musician, but as a man laid bare, stripped of his defenses and offering her a glimpse into his very soul.

The silence stretched on, but it wasn't uncomfortable. Rather, it felt like a sacred space, a moment suspended in time where the rest of the world fell away and all that existed was the two of them, connected by a bond that ran deeper than words could express.

Lottie's heart swelled with a fierce protectiveness, a desire to shield Alex from the pain of his past and the scrutiny of the world. But more than that, she felt a growing affection, a tenderness that went beyond mere friendship. She knew, instinctively, that her feelings for him had evolved into something more profound - something that both terrified and thrilled her in equal measure.

As she gazed at Alex, Lottie's mind raced with the possibilities of what could be. She imagined stolen moments of laughter and passion, lazy mornings tangled in sheets, and late nights sharing their deepest secrets and desires. The thought of exploring this new facet of their relationship sent a shiver down her spine, a delicious anticipation that she couldn't ignore.

But with the anticipation came a flicker of doubt. What if Alex didn't feel the same way? What if she was misreading the signals, seeing more than what was really there? Lottie had been hurt before, had given her heart only to have it returned in pieces. Could she risk that again, especially with someone as important to her as Alex had become?

She took a deep breath, her decision crystalizing in her mind. Life was too short to live in fear, to let the ghosts of the past dictate the choices of the present. She had to be brave, to take a chance on the possibility of something beautiful and real.

Lottie reached out, her hand trembling slightly as she intertwined her fingers with Alex's. His skin was warm and rough, a testament to the years he had spent coaxing magic from guitar strings. She met his gaze, her eyes shining with a mix of vulnerability and determination.

"Alex," she said softly, her voice barely above a whisper. "I... I think I'm falling for you. And I know it's complicated, and I know there are a million reasons why it might not work, but... I want to try. I want to see where this could go, if you're willing."

The words hung in the air between them, a declaration and a question all in one. Lottie held her breath, her heart pounding in her chest as she waited for Alex's response. Whatever happened next, she knew that she had taken a step forward, had dared to reach for something that could be the greatest adventure of her life.

eight

. . .

Hannah leaned back in her squeaky office chair, stretching her arms overhead as she surveyed the controlled chaos of her cluttered newsroom desk. Stacks of paper teetered precariously, a half-empty coffee mug leaving rings on a dog-eared notepad. Fluorescent lights buzzed overhead, mingling with the hum of computers and chatter of her fellow reporters chasing deadlines.

Her dark eyes flitted across the mess until they landed on a crumpled newspaper clipping. Smoothing it out, a name jumped off the page - Alex King. Hannah's brow furrowed. The former rock star had all but vanished from the spotlight years ago after his Grammy-winning band **"Hollow Reign"** imploded. Reclusive. Private. A mystery.

Scanning the article, one line ignited a spark in Hannah's ever-curious mind: "King has retreated behind the closed doors of **The Velvet Room**, a vintage music store shrouded in secrecy."

"Jackpot," she murmured, fingers already itching to unravel this tangled story. To discover the man behind the legend's crumbling facade. Because that's what Hannah did best - digging, probing, not stopping until all the pieces fit.

She pictured him, this Alex King. Flashes of tousled graying hair, piercing eyes that hypnotized stadiums full of screaming fans, a soulful voice now hidden away, collecting dust like the antique guitars rumored to line **The Velvet Room**' walls. *What secrets lay locked behind that faded music store door?*

"I need everything we've got on Alex King and **The Velvet Room**," Hannah called out to the intern passing by, jolting upright in her seat as the first tendrils of a relentless itch - that delicious thrill when the scent of a story hit - took hold.

Her mind raced with possibilities, avenues to investigate, locks to pick. A slow smile tugged at her lips.

It was time to blow the dust off a legend - whether he liked it or not.

* * *

HANNAH'S FINGERS flew across the keyboard, a flurry of searches and queries, each click drawing her deeper into the enigma of Alex King. Old interviews, archived articles, fan forums filled with speculation and hearsay - piece by piece, she stitched together a patchwork portrait of the man behind the music.

A troubled childhood. A meteoric rise to fame. Platinum records and sold-out tours. And then... silence. A sudden vanishing act, leaving behind only whispers and rumors.

She leaned back in her chair, eyes narrowed at the screen. "What made you disappear, Alex?" Hannah murmured, her words hanging in the stillness of the empty newsroom. "What are you hiding?"

Reaching for her phone, she scrolled through her contacts, stopping at a name that might hold the key: Liam Wright, an old college friend turned music journalist. If anyone had the inside scoop on Alex King, it would be Liam.

The phone rang once, twice. "Hey, stranger," Liam's familiar voice filled her ear. "To what do I owe the pleasure?"

"I need a favor," Hannah said, cutting straight to the chase. "What do you know about Alex King and **The Velvet Room?**"

A pause. A sharp inhale. "Why the sudden interest in a has-been rock star?"

Hannah twirled a pen between her fingers, a smirk playing on her lips. "Call it a hunch. There's a story here, Liam. I can feel it."

"Listen, Hannah..." Liam's tone turned serious. "Alex King's a tough nut to crack. He's been off the grid for years. Doesn't do interviews, doesn't play the fame game anymore."

"But you know something, don't you?" Hannah pressed, her journalist's instinct kicking into high gear. "C'mon, Liam. Help a girl out."

She could practically hear Liam's mind whirring through the phone, weighing the risks and rewards of spilling industry secrets. Finally, he sighed. "Alright, but you didn't hear this from me..."

Hannah leaned forward, pen poised over her notebook, ready to uncover the truth buried beneath the silence of a faded rock legend.

Hannah jotted down every detail Liam shared, her pen flying across the pages. Alex King's retreat from the limelight, his purchase of **The Velvet Room**, the whispers of a man seeking solace in music. With each revelation, the puzzle pieces began to fall into place.

"Thanks, Liam," Hannah said, the excitement in her voice palpable. "I owe you one."

"Just be careful, Hannah," Liam warned. "Alex King's not a man to be trifled with."

But Hannah was already disconnecting the call, her mind racing with possibilities. She glanced at the address scrawled in her notebook: **The Velvet Room**. It was time to see the enigma up close.

DETERMINATION COURSING THROUGH HER VEINS, Hannah poured over every article, every interview, every scrap of information she could find on Alex King and his reclusive years. The more she read, the more intrigued she became. There were whispers of a fallen superstar, a man who'd lost his way in the limelight, but no one knew the whole story.

As the hours ticked by, Hannah's eyelids grew heavy, but

she fought off the pull of sleep. She couldn't rest until she unraveled the enigma that was Alex King.

The next morning, armed with a fresh pot of coffee and renewed determination, Hannah hit the streets of Seattle. She spoke to everyone she could find, from baristas to bartenders, asking about the elusive musician. Some remembered him vaguely, others shook their heads, but no one had seen or heard from him in years.

Just when she was about to give up, a wrinkled old woman in the corner of the local diner perked up at the mention of Alex King. "I haven't seen him in donkey's years, but last I heard, he was holed up in his old family estate on the outskirts of town."

Hannah's heart skipped a beat. "Do you know where that is?"

HANNAH STEELED herself as she approached the entrance of **The Velvet Room**, her heart pounding with anticipation. The door chimed softly as she stepped inside, the familiar scent of new paint and nostalgia enveloping her senses.

She scanned the music venue—someone had been renovating. Her interest in him and this place revved up.

Her eyes searched for the enigmatic figure she had come to confront, but all she found was some young girl at the bar, going through receipts.

"Hi, can I help you?" Lottie asked, wondering who this woman was.

"Hi, my name is Hannah Dawson. I'm a columnist working for the magazine, **Culture Clash**. I'm looking for Alex King—I was told I would find him here?"

Lottie looked the woman up and down and she seemed legit. And anyhow, any buzz about Alex would only help her business. "His apartment is upstairs. If you go down this hall, you'll find a staircase leading up to the second and third levels. His apartment is on the left."

Hannah nodded her thanks and set off to find him.

Finding his apartment door at last, she knocked gently.

No answer—was he home?

The second knock ... the door opened, and there he was.

Alex King.

Hannah approached him cautiously, her voice steady despite the nerves coursing through her veins. "Alex King? I'm Hannah Dawson, a columnist from **Culture**

Clash. I've been researching your story, and I have some questions I'd like to ask you."

Alex turned to face her, his blue eyes piercing in their intensity. "And what makes you think I have any interest in answering them?"

"I've uncovered a lot about your past, about your reasons for leaving the music industry," Hannah pressed on, undeterred. "I believe your story deserves to be told, and I want to give you the chance to share your side."

Alex let out a low chuckle, shaking his head. "You think you have it all figured out, don't you? Another journalist looking for a scoop, eager to expose the truth behind the reclusive rock star."

Hannah met his gaze, her determination unwavering. "I'm not here for a scoop. I'm here because I believe there's more to your story than what the public knows. I want to understand what drove you to walk away from it all."

Alex studied her for a long moment, his expression unreadable. "And what if the truth isn't what you expect? What if the reality is far less glamorous than the myth?"

"That's a risk I'm willing to take," Hannah replied, her

voice softening. "I'm not here to judge or sensationalize. I just want to listen, to give you a chance to be heard."

Alex sighed, running a hand through his tousled hair. "Fine. But not here. If we're going to do this, it needs to be on my terms."

Hannah nodded, a flicker of triumph sparking within her. "Name the time and place, and I'll be there."

As Alex scribbled down an address on a slip of paper, Hannah couldn't help but feel a rush of excitement mixed with trepidation. She was on the cusp of uncovering a story that had haunted her for weeks, but at what cost?

She took the paper from Alex's hand, their fingers brushing briefly, and felt a jolt of electricity course through her. It was a touch that spoke of secrets yet to be revealed, of a connection that went beyond the professional.

Hannah tucked the address into her pocket, her mind already racing with the possibilities of what lay ahead. She knew she was walking a fine line, blurring the boundaries between journalist and subject. But as she met Alex's gaze once more, she couldn't deny the pull she felt towards him, the desire to unravel the enigma that was Alex King.

"Thank you," she said softly, her voice barely above a whisper. "I'll see you soon."

And with that, Hannah turned and walked away, the weight of the story heavy on her shoulders, but the promise of revelation spurring her forward.

nine

. . .

The soft glow of the Edison bulbs strung across **The Velvet Room** cast a warm, sepia-toned veil over the couple seated at the corner table. Lottie and Alex, their fingers entwined, spoke in hushed tones that mingled with the hum of a vinyl record spinning in the background—an old blues number that seemed to bleed into the room's woodwork.

"Place is almost ready," Alex's voice was a low murmur, his thumb gently stroking Lottie's hand. "We should talk talent."

Lottie smiled, her eyes reflecting the dim light as she squeezed his hand. "What were you thinking?" she asked, her voice carrying the weight of unspoken stories.

They sipped coffee from mismatched mugs, the steam curling like whispers between them. This was their sanctuary, cocooned away from the world, where the passage of time was marked only by the flip of a record's side.

Suddenly, the moment shattered like glass under a boot heel. The quietude was pierced by the cacophony of reporters descending upon the venue like vultures to carrion. Camera shutters clicked in rapid succession, creating a relentless staccato that jarred the senses. Shouts ricocheted off the walls, each syllable sharp and intrusive —a stark contrast to the tranquil bubble that had enveloped Lottie and Alex moments before.

"Alex King, is it true you're planning a comeback tour?" one voice cut through the din, hungry for a scoop.

"Mr. King, over here! A word about your rumored album!" another clamored, not to be outdone.

Alex's body tensed, his shoulders becoming a fortress against the intrusion. He turned to Lottie, the blue of his eyes now stormy with conflict. She could see the fortress walls in his gaze, built high from years in the public eye —walls that had once shielded him but now threatened to separate them.

Lottie's hand found Alex's, their fingers intertwining in a silent pact as the clamor swelled around them. The air felt heavy, charged with the electric hum of voices and the relentless flashing of cameras. They stood still, two souls amidst a storm of notoriety, sharing a glance that spoke volumes. In the span of a heartbeat, their haven was no longer theirs alone.

The reporters, like a flock of birds descending on an untouched field, invaded the space with an eagerness that bordered on frenzy. Their shouts were the caws and cries, each one piercing the serenity Lottie and Alex had so carefully cultivated.

And then he appeared.

Lyle Simmons emerged from behind the voracious crowd, his presence cutting through the chaos like a sleek ship parting turbulent waters. His smile was knowing, predatory; the kind of grin that suggested a chess game only he knew he was playing. He stood there, an embodiment of the industry that fed on talent and left little room for the personal.

His eyes fixed on Alex, a glint of triumph twinkling within their depths—victory lay just within reach, ripe for the taking. But Lottie's gaze held steady, her protective stance beside Alex unwavering. She could feel the weight of Lyle's scrutiny, the assessment of a man who saw people not as they were, but as pawns to be positioned and played.

In this moment of frozen time, Lottie understood with chilling clarity: their world was teetering on the precipice of change, and Lyle Simmons was the harbinger, ready to tip it all into the abyss.

Lyle advanced, weaving through the throng of reporters with the ease of a man used to navigating treacherous waters. His voice, slick as oiled leather, slid into the space between Lottie and Alex. "What a scene we have here!" he exclaimed, his arms open in feigned surprise. "Alex King, back in the limelight. Just think of it—the comeback tour, the album sales, the world waiting on your next word."

The offer hung in the air, coated in the honeyed tone of opportunity. Yet, beneath the gloss, there was the unmistakable tang of a trap snapping shut.

"Picture this," Lyle continued, his eyes locked onto Alex's, "a new era for *Hollow Reign,*' bigger than ever before." He spun words like a spider spins silk, each thread designed to ensnare and bind.

But Lottie felt the stirrings of something deep within her —a protective fire that rose from her belly and set her heart ablaze. She stepped forward, placing herself between Alex and the serpent's smile that threatened their peace.

"Thank you, Lyle, but no," she said, her voice soft yet edged with steel. Her hand found Alex's, a silent declaration of solidarity. "I'm not interested in your promises."

Lyle's eyebrows lifted slightly, the only crack in his practiced demeanor. "Now, darling, don't be hasty," he cooed, attempting to sidestep her to reach Alex. "This could change your life."

THEY SLIPPED through the back door of **The Velvet Room**, the clamor of the media storm muffled like a song played underwater. In the venue's private room, lined with shelves of old records and dimly lit by a single lamp, Lottie and Alex found their breaths syncing to the quiet rhythm of respite.

"Are you okay?" Lottie's voice was a whisper, but in the hush, it filled the space around them.

Alex ran a hand through his salt-and-pepper hair and let out a slow exhale. "I feel like I'm trapped in one of those old tracks—stuck on repeat," he admitted, the rugged lines of his face etched with conflict.

The chaos outside seemed a world away as they settled onto an aged leather couch, its surface worn smooth by countless hours of contemplation and conversation. Lottie nestled close to him, her shoulder brushing against his as she sought to share the burden of his turmoil.

"Everything is changing so fast," she said, her voice barely above the hum of the vintage turntable in the corner. "But this—us—it feels right."

He turned to look at her, the intensity of his blue eyes seeking hers in the soft light. "Lottie, if I step back into that life..." His words trailed off, a wave retreating from the shore.

"Then we face it together," she replied, her resolve solidifying like a chord struck firmly on a guitar. "We don't have to let them rewrite our song."

Their shared silence spoke volumes, a duet of uncertainty and determination. The room, with its scent of nostalgia —dusty vinyl and faded paper—seemed to envelop them, a protective cocoon from the relentless tempo of the world outside.

Alex's gaze lingered on Lottie's black hair, the way it framed her thoughtful face. "I just don't want to lose this," he said, motioning to the room, to her, to everything unspoken between them. "Or you."

"Then hold on tight," she answered, her fingers entwining with his, a tangible promise. "Sometimes the most profound songs are the ones sung softly, away from the spotlight."

With her hand in his, Alex felt the anchor of her presence, the calm amidst the storm. Outside, the media's siren call beckoned, but within these four walls, there was only the gentle crackle of a needle finding its groove, the quiet harmony of two souls navigating the score of an uncertain future.

The needle dropped, a soft hiss filling the silence before the room hummed with the gentle strumming of an acoustic guitar. Lottie watched Alex's face, the furrows in his brow deepening with each click and shout that seeped through the walls.

"Alex," she began, her voice a quiet beacon, "we can't control the circus outside. But we can decide how to dance in it." She paused, considering her words like selecting the perfect vinyl for a turntable. "Let's write our own narrative."

He looked at her, the blue of his eyes darkening like the sky before a storm. "How?" The word lingered between them, frail and uncertain.

"By being who we are," she said, simple yet profound. "We share this love for music, for **The Velvet Room**. This place..." Her gaze swept the room, lingering on the worn covers and timeless melodies encased within. "It's our melody, not theirs."

"A melody haven," he whispered, the name a vow.

"Exactly." Lottie's lips curled into a smile, small but fierce. "We'll keep creating, keep playing. On our terms. No contracts, no spotlights—just us and the music."

The idea settled around Alex like an old, familiar jacket, comforting in its fit. He could almost taste the freedom in her proposal, sweet and heady as the first chord struck on a clear morning.

"Without Lyle's strings attached?" he asked, hope threading his voice.

"Without any strings," she affirmed, her hand squeezing his. "Just the strings on our guitars."

The vision of it—a life unfettered by the clamor of fame, a duet with Lottie under the soft glow of stage lights in their sanctuary—filled Alex with a courage he hadn't known was there. His past, a cacophony of applause and demands, faded into a background hum.

"I'm in," he said, the decision ringing clear and true. "I choose this. I choose us."

LOTTIE'S FINGERS intertwined with Alex's as they stepped through the door, leaving the quiet hum of the private room behind. The chaos outside crashed against their senses like a rogue wave, reporters jostling for position, camera flashes igniting the dim corridor of **The Velvet Room**. Lottie felt Alex's grip tighten, an unspoken signal of solidarity.

"Ready?" Alex's voice was a low rumble, steady as the bass line of a forgotten classic rock anthem.

"Let's do this." Lottie's reply was barely audible over the din, her words a simple melody in a cacophony of questions and demands.

As they moved forward, the sea of bodies parted reluctantly, the air thick with anticipation. Lottie could feel the weight of every gaze upon them, the scrutiny as tangible as the vintage vinyl that lined the shelves of The Velvet Room.

"Mr. King, Ms. Madden, what do you have to say about Mr. Simmons' offer?" A reporter's voice sliced through the babel, sharp and seeking.

Alex's blue eyes met Lottie's, a silent exchange passing between them. He cleared his throat, and when he spoke, his voice carried the gravity of a man who had known the intoxicating allure of fame but now sought the quiet dignity of obscurity.

"Thank you all for your interest," Alex began, his words measured. "But we've decided not to accept Mr. Simmons' offer."

A collective intake of breath rippled through the crowd. Lyle's smugness wavered, his polished facade showing the first crack.

"May I ask why?" Another voice chimed in, eager for the morsel of scandal.

Lottie felt a surge of protectiveness rise within her, a fierce guardian of the peace they had nurtured in this sanctuary of sound. She stepped closer to Alex, her voice a soft yet resolute note that somehow soared above the uproar.

"Because what we have here is about more than fame or fortune," she said. "It's about music in its purest form.

It's about creating something real—something that isn't manufactured or manipulated by industry expectations."

The reporters scrambled, pens scratching and cameras clicking, trying desperately to capture the essence of the moment. But the truth was something ethereal, a chord struck in perfect harmony that resonated only between Lottie and Alex.

"Are you turning your back on your fans, Mr. King?" The question was pointed, a barbed hook cast into still waters.

Alex's laugh lines deepened as he smiled, a gesture tinged with the wisdom of experience. "Not at all. We're simply choosing a path that's right for us—one that allows us to connect with our fans on our terms."

The media horde seemed to falter, their thirst for salacious headlines left unquenched. Lottie glanced at Alex, pride swelling in her chest like a crescendo. They had faced the storm together and emerged not just unscathed but stronger, their resolve a lighthouse guiding them through the fog of temptation.

"Thank you, that will be all," Alex concluded, his declaration punctuating the air like the final beat of a drum solo.

Hand in hand, they turned away from the flashing cameras and probing questions. The noise faded into a distant echo, the clamor of the world rendered insignificant by the symphony of their united hearts.

ten

. . .

The sun-drenched street shimmered like a mirage as Oliver Hammond approached the music venue, his sandy blonde hair tousled by an ever-present breeze. A mischievous grin played across his lips, eyes twinkling with barely contained excitement. He paused at the entrance, hand resting on the weathered door handle.

Another day, another chance to drag Alex out of his shell, Oliver mused, chuckling softly to himself.

He pushed open the door, the familiar scent of dust and old amplifiers washing over him. The venue buzzed with activity—workers scurrying about, hauling equipment, and chattering amongst themselves. It looked as if they were setting up the venue for some kind of rehearsal.

Hmmm.... Oliver's gaze swept across the room, searching for that telltale mop of salt-and-pepper hair.

Where are you hiding, you old recluse? he thought, a mixture of fondness and exasperation coloring his inner monologue.

Oliver weaved through the crowd, nodding at a few familiar faces. The low hum of anticipation in the air was palpable, reminding him of countless gigs from their heyday. A twinge of nostalgia tugged at his heart, quickly replaced by determination.

Focus, Hammond. You're here for Alex, not a trip down memory lane.

He continued his search, eyes darting from corner to corner. The venue was a labyrinth of shadows and sudden bursts of light, making the task more challenging than he'd anticipated.

"Excuse me," Oliver called out to a passing stagehand. "You haven't seen a brooding, ridiculously handsome older gentleman around here, have you? Probably looking like he'd rather be anywhere else?"

The stagehand shook his head, hurrying off with an armful of cables. Oliver sighed, running a hand through his already messy hair.

Come on, Alex. Where the hell are you?

As Oliver rounded a stack of speakers, he finally spotted Alex lurking in a dimly lit corner, looking every bit the reluctant rock star he'd always been. A smile tugged at Oliver's lips as he made his way over, expertly dodging a crew member carrying a precarious tower of music stands.

Still hiding in the shadows, I see. Some things never change.

The closer he got, the more Oliver could see the tension in Alex's shoulders, the slight furrow of his brow. It was a familiar sight, one that spoke volumes about his friend's state of mind.

Time to snap him out of it.

With practiced ease, Oliver slipped through the last of the crowd and approached Alex from behind. He clapped a hand on his friend's shoulder, feeling the slight jump of surprise beneath his palm.

"Fancy meeting you here, stranger," Oliver quipped, his eyes twinkling with mischief as Alex turned to face him.

The momentary flash of annoyance in Alex's piercing blue eyes quickly softened to recognition, then resigned amusement. Oliver squeezed his shoulder gently, a silent reassurance passing between them.

I've got your back, old friend. Always have, always will.

Alex's lips quirked in a half-smile, the lines around his eyes crinkling slightly. "Oliver," he said, his deep voice carrying a mix of relief and wariness. "I should've known you'd find me."

Oliver grinned, leaning in conspiratorially. "What can I say? I've got a sixth sense for brooding rock stars in need of a good talking-to."

Alex couldn't help but chuckle, the sound rusty from disuse. "Is that what this is? A talking-to?"

Oliver's eyes scanned the bustling venue, taking in the chaos of the renovations. "Let's find somewhere a bit quieter, shall we? Unless you're enjoying being a human obstacle course for the construction crew."

With a slight nod, Oliver followed Alex as they weaved through the maze of equipment and workers. The cacophony of power tools and shouted instructions faded as they made their way to a secluded corner near the back of the venue.

Why am I even here? Alex wondered, his mind drifting to

Lottie and the unexpected connection they'd forged. *I should be running in the opposite direction.*

They settled against a wall, the exposed brick cool against Alex's back. He could smell sawdust and fresh paint, a strange mix of destruction and rebirth that seemed oddly fitting.

"So," Oliver began, his voice lowered but still carrying that characteristic hint of amusement, "Lyle Simmons contacted me."

"I knew it," Alex mocked. "Bastard."

"He's offered the moon, Alex. A second chance—I've reached out to the other guys and they're all on board."

"And you want me on board too?" Alex asked, with a pit in his stomach.

"Hollow Reign isn't a band without it's lead singer," Oliver said, plainly.

Alex ran a hand through his salt-and-pepper hair, buying time. "It's not that simple, Ollie."

"It never is with you, mate," Oliver replied, his tone softening. "But I'm here, and I've got nowhere else to be. So spill."

The air between them grew heavy, charged with unspoken memories. Alex's gaze drifted to the old guitar cases stacked in the corner of the venue, relics of a past that still haunted him.

"You remember Stockholm?" Oliver asked, his voice low and gravelly.

Alex winced. "How could I forget? The night everything fell apart."

"Yeah, but it's also the night you wrote 'Midnight Echoes,'" Oliver countered. "Your best song, born from your darkest moment."

The weight of their shared history pressed down on Alex's chest. He could almost hear the roar of the crowd, smell the acrid scent of smoke machines, feel the sting of shattered glass on his knuckles.

"I'm not that person anymore, Ollie," Alex murmured, running a hand through his salt-and-pepper hair.

Oliver leaned in, his eyes intense. "No, you're not. You're better. Wiser. But you still deserve happiness, Alex. Don't let fear rob you of a chance at something real."

Alex's mind whirled. Images of Lottie's smile, her gentle touch on an old record, the way she hummed along to forgotten melodies - they all blended with memories of screaming fans and backstage chaos.

"What if I fuck it up?" he whispered, voicing his deepest fear.

"Then you fuck it up," Oliver shrugged. "But at least you'll have tried. And who knows? Maybe this time, the music will be sweeter for the risk."

Alex felt a flutter in his chest, a spark of something he hadn't felt in years. Hope, maybe? Or just the terrifying thrill of possibility.

Oliver's lips curved into a knowing smile. "I see those gears turning, old man. Remember, life's not a dress rehearsal. Sometimes you gotta jump in and play the damn song, even if you're not sure of all the chords."

"Easy for you to say," Alex grumbled, but there was no real bite to his words. "You've always been the risk-taker."

"And you've always been the one with the most to gain," Oliver countered. He stood up, stretching his lean frame. "Look, I'm not saying it'll be easy. But think about it - when was the last time you felt truly alive? Truly inspired?"

The question hung in the air, heavy with implication. Alex's mind drifted to Lottie, to the way her eyes lit up when she talked about music, to the electricity he felt when their fingers brushed over a vinyl sleeve.

Oliver placed a hand on Alex's shoulder, giving it a firm squeeze. "Just... don't let fear be the thing that writes your story, yeah?"

Alex slowly nodded his head, yes.

Oliver smiled, "Yeah? Are we doing this? We're getting the band back together?"

Alex smiled, and swallowed hard.

"Awesome! I'm off to see Lyle," Oliver said, grinning from ear to ear.

As they moved to part ways, Oliver gave Alex a reassuring pat on the back. No words were needed; the gesture spoke volumes. A promise of support, a reminder of their unbreakable bond.

Alex watched his friend weave through the crowded venue, feeling a mix of gratitude and trepidation. The path ahead was uncertain, but for the first time in years, he felt ready to take that first step.

Alex's eyes lingered on Oliver's retreating form, his friend's tousled blonde hair disappearing into the crowd like the last notes of a favorite song. A surge of gratitude washed over him, mingling with a newfound determination that set his heart racing.

He ran a hand through his salt-and-pepper locks, exhaling slowly. "Alright, old man," he muttered to himself. "Time to stop hiding."

With each step towards Lottie, memories of past failures and regrets threatened to drown him. But Oliver's words echoed in his mind, a lifeline in the storm of his thoughts.

As he approached, Alex caught sight of Lottie bent over a box of records, her black hair falling like a curtain around her face. The sight of her sent a jolt through his system, equal parts exhilaration and terror.

"Hey," he called out, his deep voice barely audible over the bustling activity around them.

Lottie looked up, her warm brown eyes widening in surprise. "Alex! I thought you'd left."

He shook his head, a wry smile tugging at his lips. "Nah, just... processing. Listen, I was wondering if we could talk. Maybe grab a coffee?"

Lottie hesitated, and Alex felt his heart skip a beat. *Was he too late?* Had he pushed her away one too many times?

"I'd like that," she finally said, her soft voice carrying a hint of hope.

As they made their way out of the venue, Alex felt lighter than he had in years. The future was uncertain, but for once, he was ready to face it head-on.

Alex held the door open for Lottie, the cool breeze outside a stark contrast to the stuffy atmosphere of the venue. As they stepped onto the sidewalk, their shoulders brushed, sending a spark of electricity through Alex's body.

"There's a little café around the corner," Lottie suggested, gesturing down the street. "They make a mean latte."

Alex nodded, falling into step beside her. "Sounds perfect."

The walk was short but charged with unspoken tension. Alex's mind raced, trying to find the right words to express the tumult of emotions inside him.

"So," Lottie began, breaking the silence. "What did you want to talk about?"

Alex took a deep breath. "I... I wanted to apologize. For being so distant. For pushing you away."

Lottie's eyes met his, a mixture of surprise and caution in their depths. "Oh?"

They reached the café, pausing outside its quaint storefront. Alex ran a hand through his hair, a nervous habit he'd never quite shaken.

"I've been scared, Lottie. Terrified, actually. Of feeling... of connecting with someone again."

Lottie's expression softened. "Alex, I—"

"No, please. Let me finish," he interrupted gently. "You've awakened something in me, something I thought was long dead. And it scares the hell out of me."

As they stood there, the world seemed to fade away. It was just them, caught in a moment of raw honesty. Alex's heart pounded in his chest, each beat a reminder of how alive he felt in Lottie's presence.

Lottie reached out, her fingers grazing his arm. "I'm scared too, you know. This isn't exactly familiar territory for me either."

Alex chuckled, the sound low and warm. "Look at us. A couple of scared kids pretending to be adults."

Lottie's laugh joined his, the sound like music to his ears. As their laughter subsided, their eyes met once more. At that moment, something shifted. The air between them crackled with possibility, with promise.

Without thinking, Alex leaned in slightly, drawn by an invisible force. Lottie mirrored his movement, her eyes never leaving his. The world held its breath as they stood on the precipice of something new, something profound.

And in that meaningful glance, strengthened by Oliver's support and their own courage, Alex and Lottie found a connection that transcended words. The chapter of uncertainty closed, and a new one, filled with hope and potential, began to unfold.

eleven

. . .

The ticking of the ancient clock on the wall seemed to echo Lottie's racing heartbeat. Her fingers drummed an erratic rhythm on the worn wooden counter, each tap sending tiny vibrations through her body. The scent of musty books and vinyl mingled in the air, a familiar comfort that did little to soothe her churning thoughts.

Alex's face floated in her mind, those piercing blue eyes that had seen so much, the salt-and-pepper hair she longed to run her fingers through. *God, what was she thinking?* He was older, experienced, a literal rock legend. And she was just... Lottie. Plain, shy, bookish Lottie.

She sighed, her gaze drifting to the vinyl display. A **Hollow Reign** album stared back at her, Alex's younger self frozen in time on the cover. The irony wasn't lost on her.

The bell above the door jingled, shattering her reverie. Lottie's head snapped up, her heart leaping, but it wasn't Alex.

Cassie burst into **The Velvet Room** like a whirlwind of energy, her fiery red hair a beacon in the dim store. "Lottie, darling! I brought coffee and— wait, what's wrong?"

Lottie blinked, realizing she must look as distracted as she felt. "Nothing's wrong," she lied, forcing a smile. "Just... thinking."

Cassie's green eyes narrowed, seeing right through her. She set two coffee cups on the counter and leaned in, her voice dropping conspiratorially. "Bullshit. You've got that deer-in-headlights look. Spill."

Lottie hesitated, her fingers now fidgeting with a loose thread on her vintage sweater. How could she even begin to explain the tornado of emotions swirling inside her?

Lottie took a deep breath, the scent of old vinyl and Cassie's vanilla perfume mingling in the air. "It's... it's Alex," she finally admitted, her voice barely above a whisper.

Cassie's eyebrows shot up, a grin spreading across her face. "Oh? Do tell!"

Lottie's cheeks flushed, and she looked down at her hands. "I have so much goin' on, ya know?"

Cassie nodded her head, yes. "I know—I know."

Lottie continued, "…and Alex, well, he's thinking about getting his band back together."

Cassie shook her head, "Oh, that's great! But why the sour look?"

Lottie shook her head, "Oh Cass…I think I'm… developing feelings for him. But God, Cassie, it's crazy, right? He's so much older, and he's been through so much. What could he possibly see in someone like me?"

The words tumbled out like a flood, all her fears and insecurities laid bare. She glanced up, half-expecting to see judgment in Cassie's eyes. Instead, she found nothing but warmth and understanding.

Cassie reached across the counter, grabbing Lottie's hand. "Oh, honey," she said softly, her usual exuberance tempered by genuine empathy. "There's nothing crazy about it. Alex would be lucky to have you."

Lottie shook her head, unconvinced. "But the age difference... and he's practically a celebrity. I'm just... me."

"Just you?" Cassie squeezed her hand. "Lottie, you're amazing. And trust me, I've seen the way he looks at you. That man is smitten."

A flutter of hope stirred in Lottie's chest, quickly quashed by doubt. "Even if he is... what if I'm not enough? What if I'm too inexperienced, too boring?"

Cassie's green eyes softened. "Listen to me, Charlotte Madden. It's okay to be scared. Taking a leap of faith in love is terrifying. But you can't let fear hold you back from something that could be beautiful."

Cassie's lips quirked into a mischievous smile. "You know, this reminds me of the time I fell for that brooding barista at Midnight Roast." She waggled her eyebrows, coaxing a reluctant grin from Lottie.

"Oh God, not Jake the Java Jerk," Lottie groaned, but her eyes sparkled with curiosity.

"The very same," Cassie said, dramatically flipping her fiery hair. "There I was, pining over his perfectly foam-etched lattes and chiseled jawline for weeks. Finally, I decided to shoot my shot."

Lottie leaned in, momentarily forgetting her own troubles. "And?"

"I marched up to that counter, looked him dead in the eye, and said—" Cassie paused for effect, "'I'll have a venti... you.'"

A burst of laughter escaped Lotte, echoing through the cozy confines of the venue. "You did not!"

"Oh, but I did," Cassie grinned. "And you know what? It worked. We dated for six glorious, caffeine-fueled months."

Lottie's smile faded slightly. "But it didn't last."

"No, it didn't," Cassie agreed, her tone softening. "But I don't regret it for a second. Life's too short to wonder 'what if,' Lottie."

The words hung in the air, heavy with meaning. Lottie gnawed her lower lip, her fingers absently tracing the grooves of a nearby vinyl record. "But what if I mess everything up?" she whispered.

Cassie's gaze was steady, her voice firm but gentle. "Then you pick yourself up and try again. But Lottie, honey, you've got to trust your instincts. That little voice inside telling you to go for it? Listen to it." Cassie leaned forward, her green eyes intense with sincerity. "Lottie, you're one of the strongest people I know. You've weathered so much already - inheriting this place, rebuilding your life. And look at what you've done with **The Velvet Room!**"

Lottie glanced around the venue, taking in the carefully curated shelves and the soft glow of vintage lamps. A faint smile tugged at her lips.

"You've got this resilience in you," Cassie continued, her voice thick with emotion. "It's like... it's like one of those old vinyl records you love so much. They might get scratched, but they keep playing, you know? That's you, Lottie."

Lottie's chest tightened, a warmth spreading through her.

"And happiness? Fulfillment? You deserve every bit of it," Cassie said, reaching out to squeeze Lottie's hand. "Don't let fear hold you back from something that could be amazing."

As Cassie's words sank in, Lottie felt something shift inside her. The doubts that had been swirling like a discordant melody began to fade, replaced by a growing sense of determination. She straightened her shoulders, meeting Cassie's gaze with newfound resolve.

Lottie's eyes welled up with emotion, her heart swelling with gratitude. She reached out and squeezed Cassie's hand tightly. "Cassie, I... I don't know what I'd do without you," she said, her voice wavering slightly. "You've always been here for me, through everything. Our friendship... it means more to me than I can say."

Cassie's eyes sparkled with warmth as she returned the squeeze. "That's what best friends are for, silly," she replied with a gentle smile.

Lottie took a deep breath, her mind racing. The familiar scent of old vinyl and paper surrounded her, grounding her in the moment. She glanced at the **Hollow Reign** poster on the wall, Alex's piercing blue eyes seeming to look right through her.

"I think..." Lottie began, her voice barely above a whisper. She cleared her throat and tried again, stronger this time. "I think I'm going to go for it with Alex."

As the words left her mouth, Lottie felt a surge of exhilaration course through her body. Her face lit up, a genuine smile spreading across her features. It was as if a weight had been lifted off her shoulders, replaced by a newfound confidence.

"Life's too short to let opportunities pass by, right?"

Lottie said, her brown eyes shining with determination. "I want to see where this could go."

Cassie let out an excited squeal, her fiery red hair bouncing as she jumped up and down. "That's my girl!" she exclaimed, holding up her hand for a high-five. "Come on, don't leave me hanging!"

Lottie laughed, the sound light and carefree, as she slapped her palm against Cassie's. The sharp clap echoed through the store, mingling with the soft strains of a classic rock ballad playing in the background.

"I promise you, Lottie," Cassie said, her tone suddenly serious despite the mischievous glint in her green eyes, "I'll be right here for you every step of the way. Through the butterflies, the awkward silences, and even if you need me to hide in the bushes during your first date."

Lottie rolled her eyes, but couldn't suppress her grin. "I think I can manage without a spy, thanks."

As Cassie gathered her things to leave, Lottie felt a renewed sense of purpose coursing through her veins. She ran her fingers along the spine of a nearby vinyl record, its worn edges a testament to the passage of time.

"You've got this," Cassie called over her shoulder as she

headed for the door. "Remember, you're Charlotte freaking Madden, and you're about to rock Alex's world!"

The bell above the door jingled as Cassie left, leaving Lottie alone with her thoughts. She leaned against the counter, her mind racing with possibilities. The challenges ahead seemed less daunting now, overshadowed by the excitement of what could be.

"I'm ready," Lottie whispered to herself, a quiet affirmation in the stillness of the store. She glanced once more at Alex's poster, her heart skipping a beat. "Bring on the adventure."

twelve

. . .

lex's fingers moved across the guitar strings, each note a piece of his heart poured onto the page. The small table tucked in the corner of his apartment was littered with crumpled sheets, discarded lyrics that couldn't capture what he needed to say. What he needed her to hear.

He closed his eyes, letting the melody guide him. Memories of Lottie danced behind his eyelids - the shy smile that lit up her face when she talked about her favorite bands, the way her eyes sparkled when she laughed at one of his terrible jokes. She'd walked into his life and woken up parts of him he thought were long dead, parts he'd buried under the debris of fame and heartbreak.

The lyrics flowed from someplace deep inside, words he could never bring himself to say out loud. Alex had always been better with a guitar in his hands, the strings a mouthpiece for his soul.

"I never knew what I was missin', until your eyes met mine..." His husky voice, weathered by age and too many cigarettes, carried through the empty venue. "You're bringing me back to life, baby, in ways I can't define..."

God, if his former bandmates could see him now - Alex King, the once great rock god, stripped down to his rawest form. Bleeding his heart out over a woman nearly half his age. They'd never let him live it down.

But Lottie was different. She looked at him and saw beyond the wrinkles and faded tattoos, beyond the platinum records and Rolling Stone covers gathering dust on the shelf. She saw him. The real him. And that both terrified and thrilled him in equal measure.

His calloused fingers danced across the fretboard with an intensity that matched the emotion pulsing through his veins. The song built to a crescendo, the final notes ringing out into the silence.

Alex opened his eyes and stared down at the messy scrawl. It was rough, but it was real. Just like what he felt for her. He knew in his bones that Lottie was his second chance, his shot at a love he never thought he deserved.

And tonight, in front of the whole damn world, he was going to make sure she knew it too.

LOTTIE STEPPED into the dimly lit room, the floorboards creaking softly beneath her boots. Her breath caught in her throat as her eyes landed on Alex, hunched over his guitar in the corner. She paused, drinking in the sight of him lost in his music, his brow furrowed in concentration.

The melody wrapped around her like a warm embrace, the notes aching with a vulnerability she'd never heard from him before. It tugged at something deep inside her, urging her closer.

She hesitated, torn between the desire to be near him and the fear of shattering the magic of the moment. Her heart raced as she watched his fingers dance across the strings, coaxing out a haunting refrain that resonated in her very soul.

God, what was he doing to her? This man, with his weathered hands and gravelly voice, had turned her world upside down from the moment he'd walked into **The**

Velvet Room. She'd tried to keep her distance, to guard her heart, but it was a losing battle.

Lottie's feet moved of their own accord, drawn to him like a moth to a flame. She needed to be closer, to feel the heat of his skin and breathe in the scent of leather and smoke that clung to him like a second skin.

But still, she held back. This was his moment, his creation. She had no right to intrude, no matter how badly she ached to be a part of it. So she hovered at the edge of the shadows, her lips parted in silent awe as she watched him pour his heart out onto the page.

It was the most beautiful thing she'd ever seen.

Lottie took a deep breath, summoning every ounce of courage she possessed. "Alex?" Her voice was barely a whisper, but in the stillness of the room, it seemed to echo like a thunderclap.

Alex's head snapped up, his eyes meeting hers with an intensity that stole the breath from her lungs. For a moment, they simply stared at each other, the air between them crackling with an electric current that sent shivers down her spine.

Then, slowly, a smile spread across Alex's face, warming his features like the first rays of dawn. He set the guitar aside and rose to his feet, his movements fluid and graceful despite the years that had passed since his rock star days.

"Lottie," he murmured, her name a caress on his lips. "I didn't hear you come in."

She swallowed hard, her mouth suddenly dry. "I didn't want to interrupt. It sounded... beautiful."

Alex's smile widened, his eyes crinkling at the corners. "Thank you. It's not finished yet, but... it's getting there."

He took a step towards her, his hand outstretched. Lottie's heart skipped a beat as she placed her hand in his, her skin tingling at the contact. His fingers were rough and callused, a testament to the years he'd spent with a guitar in his hands.

But there was a gentleness there too, a tenderness that belied the hard edges of his rock star persona. He drew her closer, his other hand coming to rest at the small of her back.

Lottie's breath caught in her throat as she looked up at him, their faces mere inches apart. She could see the flecks of gold in his blue eyes, the faint lines that mapped the corners of his mouth.

God, he was beautiful. Not in the way of the glossy magazine covers or the airbrushed music videos, but in a raw, visceral way that spoke to something primal inside her.

She wanted to touch him, to trace the contours of his face with her fingertips and feel the rasp of his stubble against her skin. But she held back, unsure of herself in the face of his quiet intensity.

"I'm glad you're here," Alex said softly, his thumb brushing over the back of her hand. "There's something I want to show you."

Alex led Lottie downstairs to the music venue, his hand never leaving hers. The air was thick with anticipation, the soft glow of the lights casting shadows across their faces.

Lottie's heart raced as they approached the stage, a single spotlight illuminating the empty space. She could feel the heat of Alex's body beside her, the subtle scent of his cologne mingling with the musty smell of old vinyl.

"What are you doing?" she whispered, her eyes wide with wonder.

"Sit here," Alex replied, a hint of a smile playing at the corners of his mouth. "It's a surprise."

He guided her to a seat in the front row, his fingers intertwining with hers as they settled in. Lottie's skin tingled at the contact, a shiver running down her spine.

She couldn't take her eyes off him, the way the light played across the angles of his face, the intensity in his gaze as he looked out at the empty stage.

In that moment, nothing else mattered. Not the age difference between them, not the expectations of the world outside. There was only the two of them, lost in a moment that felt like it could stretch on forever.

Alex squeezed her hand, a silent reassurance that he was there with her. Lottie squeezed back, a smile tugging at her lips.

She didn't know what the future held, but she knew that she wanted to face it with him by her side. Two lonely souls, finding solace in each other's company.

The stage beckoned, a blank canvas waiting to be filled with the magic of their connection. Lottie held her breath, ready to be swept away by the music and the man who had captured her heart.

Alex took a deep breath, his piercing blue eyes never leaving Lottie's. The air crackled with anticipation as he strummed the first chords of the song, the melody filling the intimate space and capturing her attention.

The music washed over Lottie, each note a gentle caress against her skin. She couldn't look away from Alex, his rugged features softened by the glow of the spotlight, his salt-and-pepper hair falling in tousled waves around his face.

As the lyrics poured from his lips, Lottie felt her eyes well up with tears. The words spoke directly to her soul, a message of love and understanding that she had never dared to hope for.

She was completely captivated by the song, her emotions overwhelming her. It was as if Alex had reached inside her heart and put all of her deepest desires into words.

Lottie's fingers tightened around Alex's, a lifeline in the sea of feelings that threatened to drown her. She couldn't remember ever feeling so seen, so understood.

The world around them faded away, leaving only the two of them and the music that bound them together. Lottie's heart raced in her chest, her breath catching in her throat.

She had never believed in love at first sight, but in that moment, she knew that what she felt for Alex was real. It was a connection that transcended age and circumstance, a bond forged in the fires of their shared passion for music.

As the final notes of the song faded away, Lottie couldn't hold back the tears any longer. They streamed down her face, a silent testament to the power of Alex's words.

She looked up at him, her eyes shining with a mixture of gratitude and love. In that moment, she knew that her life would never be the same again.

Alex had given her the greatest gift of all - the gift of his heart, laid bare in the lyrics of a song that would stay with her forever.

thirteen

. . .

*B*ack upstairs, in his apartment, Alex's fingers brushed against her own, and Lottie felt the contact like a jolt of electricity down her spine. His hand was warm, reassuring in its strength, encasing hers with an intimate familiarity that belied the newness of their bond. Their eyes met, blue clashing with brown, and within those depths, they discovered a silent yearning tethered to a quiet hope.

Then, as if the song itself orchestrated their fate, Lottie leaned forward. Her lips, hesitant yet hungry for contact, found Alex's—a lightning strike, quiet but powerful. The spark was immediate, a flame kindled from the tinder of their combined yearnings.

Their kiss, a collision of past regrets and future dreams, ignited something deeper than either anticipated. It was a conflagration of souls, a melding of histories and hopes. The world, with its relentless march of time and tides, stilled for them in that instant, acknowledging the gravity of their union.

Lottie's mind, once a haven for solitude and reflection, now roared with a singular thought—Alex. His presence, a beacon in the labyrinth of her self-discovery, drew her irrevocably closer. This touch, this fusion of breath and being, was the answer to questions she hadn't dared to ask.

"Charlotte," Alex whispered, the name a prayer on his lips that sent shivers cascading down her spine.

"Alex," she breathed in return, the word less a name and more a key unlocking every door she had ever closed.

They were a tangle of limbs and longing, a mess of want and need.

"Are you sure?" he asked, breath hot on her neck, a whisper of concern amidst the tempest of their passion.

"Yes," she replied, her voice steady even as her body trembled with fervor.

Lottie's palms traced the contours of Alex's back, every muscle a verse in the song of his life. His hands, those sculptors of sound and masters of strings, now explored the softness of her dress, finding the zipper with an ease that whispered of his familiarity with delicate things. The fabric whispered to the floor, a fallen shroud of her former inhibitions.

"Beautiful," he murmured, his voice a low melody that resonated within the hollows of her soul. Lottie felt the word more than she heard it, a vibration against her skin where his breath touched.

"Alex," she whispered, her voice a fragile tether in the expanse of sensation. There was a question in her call, a hesitation born from a life spent in the margins.

"Let go, Lottie," he assured her, his deep voice grounding her even as they soared. "I've got you."

Their mouths locked in a passionate kiss, tongues dancing together in a rhythm as old as time. Lottie's fingers threaded through Alex's hair, pulling him closer as if trying to merge their bodies into one. She could feel his arousal pressing against her, and it sent a thrill down her spine.

Without breaking their kiss, Alex's hands traveled down Lottie's body, caressing her curves with a possessive hunger. He cupped her breast, thumb brushing over the hardened nipple, eliciting a soft moan from her lips. Heat pooled between her legs, and her hips instinctively pushed forward, seeking friction against his thigh.

Alex responded by sliding his hand down her stomach, tracing the waistband of her panties before slipping beneath the fabric. His fingers found her wet and ready, and he groaned at the feel of her slick folds. He teased her clit with gentle circles, increasing pressure and speed as Lottie's breaths grew ragged.

"Fuck, you're so wet for me," he whispered against her ear, sending shivers down her spine.

"Please, Alex," she begged, grinding against his hand. "I need more."

He obliged, slipping two fingers inside her while continuing to rub her clit with his thumb. Lottie gasped, her walls clenching around him as he pumped in and out with a slow, steady rhythm. She could feel her orgasm building, coiling tight in her belly like a spring ready to snap.

But Alex wasn't done with her yet. He broke away from their kiss, leaving her gasping for air as he trailed his lips down her neck. He sucked and bit at the sensitive skin, sending jolts of pleasure coursing through her veins.

Lottie's hands clutched at his shoulders, nails digging into his flesh as she tried to anchor herself against the onslaught of sensations.

Alex knelt in front of her, hooking his fingers into the waistband of her panties and tugging them down her legs. He tossed them aside, then spread her thighs wide, exposing her swollen sex to his gaze. He groaned, low and deep in his chest, before leaning forward and pressing a kiss to her inner thigh.

Lottie whimpered, her hips bucking involuntarily at the contact. She could feel his hot breath against her sopping wet folds, and it drove her wild with desire. Alex chuckled, the sound vibrating against her skin and sending another wave of pleasure crashing over her.

He dragged his tongue up her slit, lapping at her juices like a man starved. Lottie's hands flew to his hair, holding him in place as he feasted on her. He sucked and licked at her clit, sending sparks of electricity shooting through her body. She was so close, teetering on the edge of release, but Alex seemed determined to draw it out.

Just when she thought she couldn't take anymore, he slid two fingers back inside her, curling them upwards to hit that sweet spot deep within. Lottie screamed, her orgasm crashing over her like a tidal wave. It shook her to her core, leaving her trembling and breathless.

Alex didn't give her a chance to recover. He stood up, quickly undoing his pants and freeing his rock-hard cock. He guided himself to her entrance, then thrust inside with one powerful stroke. Lottie cried out, her body stretching to accommodate his size.

Alex set a punishing rhythm, pounding into her with an intensity that bordered on feral. She could feel every inch of him, filling her up and hitting all the right spots. She met him thrust for thrust, their bodies moving in perfect sync.

The room was filled with the sounds of their passion — the slap of skin on skin, their ragged breaths, and the wet sounds of their bodies coming together. It was primal and raw, a testament to their unbridled lust.

With each thrust, Alex hit deeper, sending shockwaves of pleasure rippling through Lottie's body. She could feel another orgasm building, stronger than before. She clung to him, nails digging into his back as she tried to hold on.

"Come for me, baby," Alex growled in her ear. "I want to feel you tighten around me."

His words sent her over the edge. Lottie came hard, screaming his name as her body convulsed around him. Alex followed soon after, groaning as he emptied himself inside her.

They collapsed onto the couch, sweaty and spent. Lottie curled up against Alex's chest, his arms wrapped tightly around her. Their breathing slowed, matching each other's rhythm as they drifted off to sleep, sated and satisfied.

"Stay with me tonight," Alex whispered, his invitation carrying the weight of a promise rather than a question.

"Always," Lottie affirmed, her response less a word and more a vow.

fourteen

. . .

The sleek black town car glided to a stop in front of *Serafina*, the city's most exclusive Italian eatery. Alex stepped out onto the bustling sidewalk, his worn leather boots a stark contrast to the polished dress shoes of the well-heeled patrons streaming past. He took a deep breath, inhaling the savory aromas of garlic and tomato sauce mingling with expensive perfume and cologne.

As Alex approached the entrance, the heavy wooden door swung open. "Mr. King, welcome. Your party is expecting you." The maître d' gave a slight bow, ushering him inside.

The restaurant was all gleaming marble and gilded accents, with plush red velvet banquettes and crisp white tablecloths. Lyle was already seated at a corner table, sipping a glass of red wine. He stood to greet Alex, flashing a brilliantly white smile. "Alex, so good to see you again. Please, have a seat."

Alex slid into the booth, his stomach twisting into a knot. Being back in Lyle's world - the glitz, the glamour, the games - made him feel like a wolf in sheep's clothing. Or was it the other way around? He wasn't sure anymore.

"I took the liberty of ordering for us. I hope you don't mind," Lyle said smoothly, signaling the waiter. "The veal chop here is divine."

"Thanks," Alex mumbled, distracted by the gold record plaque hanging on the wall across from their table. *Hollow Reign*, it read. His band. His life, once upon a time. Before everything went to hell.

Lyle must have caught him staring. "You miss it, don't you? The rush of performing, the roar of the crowd. There's nothing else like it."

Alex tore his gaze away, focusing on the heavy silver cutlery. "I'm not that person anymore, Lyle. I've changed."

"Have you?" Lyle leaned forward, his ice-blue eyes

piercing. "A tiger can't change his stripes, Alex. Music is in your blood. It's who you are."

The waiter appeared with their food, momentarily halting the conversation. As Alex cut into the tender veal, his mind spun. Lyle's words had struck a chord. Making music had been like breathing to him once. *Could he really turn his back on that forever? Build a life, a future, with Lottie based on a lie?*

He thought of her smile, her laugh, the way she looked at him like he had hung the moon. With her, Alex felt seen, understood in a way he never had before.

But the siren song of the stage still called to him, a seductive whisper he couldn't quite shake. Memories of sweat-soaked nights under the lights, fingers flying across guitar strings, the visceral connection with a sea of fans, played through his head in vivid technicolor.

His thoughts warred as he mechanically made his way through the meal, barely registering Lyle's idle chatter. When the plates were cleared, Lyle fixed him with a penetrating stare, his geniality fading.

"Well, Alex? What's it going to be? Are you ready to stop hiding and be who you were always meant to be? The world is waiting for you, if you're ready to take the stage again."

Alex's pulse pounded in his ears, his future - two starkly divergent paths - stretching out before him. He knew, with sudden clarity, that the decision he made in this moment would shape the rest of his life. For better or for worse.

"I'm gonna pass," Alex plainly said to Lyle's shock. "I've met someone who has detoured me another way."

Lyle's smile fades slightly, a flicker of disappointment crossing his features before he quickly regains his composure. "I understand, Alex," he says, his voice smooth and measured. "It's a brave decision, prioritizing anonymity over fame. Not many in this industry would have the courage to walk away from such an opportunity."

He leans back in his chair, studying Alex with a calculating gaze. "But I feel compelled to remind you of the doors this could open, the impact you could make on the music world once again. Your talent is a rare gift, Alex. It would be a shame to let it fade into obscurity."

Alex feels a twinge of doubt, the allure of the stage tugging at his heart. But he pushes it aside, focusing on the love and stability he's found with Lottie. "I appreciate your concern, Lyle, but I've made my decision. My music will always be a part of me, but it doesn't define me anymore. I'm ready to embrace a new chapter in my life."

Lyle nods slowly, a hint of regret in his eyes. "Very well, Alex. I respect your choice, even if I don't fully agree with it. But know that the offer will remain open, should you ever change your mind. The world of rock and roll will always welcome you back with open arms."

Alex rises from his seat, a sense of finality in his movements. "Thank you, Lyle, for everything. But I'm confident in the path I've chosen. Lottie and I, we've found something real and lasting. That's what matters most to me now."

With a polite nod, Alex turns and makes his way out of the restaurant, his footsteps echoing on the polished floor. As he steps into the bustling city street, a cool breeze whips through his hair, carrying with it the faint strains of a familiar melody.

Alex's mind is a whirlwind of emotions as he walks, the gravity of his decision settling upon him. The promise of sold-out shows and screaming fans still whispers in his ear, a siren song of temptation. But the thought of Lottie, her warm smile and loving embrace, anchors him to the present.

He knows he's made the right choice, even as the allure of fame and fortune tugs at the edges of his consciousness. In Lottie, he's found a love that transcends the fleeting thrills of the stage, a connection that fills the void left by the emptiness of celebrity.

As Alex navigates the crowded sidewalks, his heart swells with a newfound sense of purpose. He may have turned his back on the bright lights of stardom, but he's embraced something far more precious: a chance at true happiness, a life built on love and authenticity.

fifteen

. . .

Alex leaned back on the worn leather couch, his fingers absentmindedly picking at a frayed seam. The dim lights of the backstage lounge cast shadows across his furrowed brow. Lottie sat beside him, the silence between them heavy with unspoken thoughts.

She reached out, her delicate hand gently resting on his. "Hey," she said softly, her warm brown eyes seeking his. "Talk to me, Alex. What's going on in that head of yours?"

He met her gaze, a wry smile tugging at the corners of his mouth. "Just thinking about how I got here. To this moment, with you."

Lottie gave his hand a reassuring squeeze. "I'm here to

listen, no matter what." Her voice was a soothing balm to his troubled mind.

Alex sighed, his shoulders sagging under the weight of his past. Images flashed through his mind - screaming fans, flashing lights, nameless faces in smoky green rooms. The rush of adrenaline, the hollow ache of loneliness.

"I'm just...tired, Lottie. Tired of running from my demons." His voice was raw, tinged with a vulnerability he rarely showed.

She scooted closer, her thigh pressing against his. "You don't have to run anymore, Alex. We can face them together."

Her words wrapped around him like a warm embrace. For the first time in years, he felt a flicker of hope. Maybe, just maybe, he could find a new path. One that led to something real and lasting.

"I don't know what I did to deserve you," he murmured, brushing a stray lock of hair from her face. "But I'm sure as hell glad you're here."

Lottie smiled, her eyes shining with adoration. "There's nowhere else I'd rather be."

Alex drew in a deep breath, steeling himself for the conversation ahead. His eyes searched Lottie's face for any sign of doubt or hesitation, but he found only unwavering support and understanding. The words tumbled from his lips, his voice low and steady.

"Lyle came to me with an offer. A chance to get back in the game, to taste that fame and fortune again." He paused, gauging her reaction. "He wants me to go on tour, to resurrect Hollow Reign for a new generation."

Lottie listened intently, her brow furrowed in concentration. She absorbed every word, her mind working to unravel the complexities of the situation. When Alex finished, she took a moment to gather her thoughts before speaking.

"What do you want, Alex? Deep down, in your heart of hearts, what do you truly desire?" Her voice was gentle but firm, urging him to look within himself for the answer.

Alex's gaze drifted to the floor, his thoughts swirling like leaves caught in a whirlwind. The allure of the stage, the roar of the crowd, the thrill of creation - it all beckoned to him like a siren's song. But beneath that, a quieter voice whispered of contentment, of lazy mornings spent wrapped in Lottie's arms, of shared laughter and inside jokes.

"I don't know," he admitted, his voice barely above a whisper. "Part of me wants to grab this chance, to prove that I've still got it. But another part of me..." He trailed off, his eyes meeting hers with an intensity that stole her breath.

Lottie leaned in, her hand coming to rest on his chest, feeling the steady thump of his heart beneath her palm. "Tell me about that other part, Alex. The part that hesitates, that questions."

He covered her hand with his own, his thumb tracing gentle circles on her skin. "That part of me knows that I've found something real here, with you. Something I never had before, even at the height of my fame. And I'm terrified of losing that."

Alex's mind drifted back to the glory days, the memories vivid and bittersweet. The deafening cheers of the crowd, the blinding lights, the rush of adrenaline as he commanded the stage - it was a high like no other. But there was a darker side to that life, one that had left scars both visible and invisible.

"I remember the endless nights on the road, the parties that blurred into one another," he said, his voice tinged with melancholy. "The pressure to be 'on' all the time, to live up to this image of the rock god. It was exhausting. And lonely."

Lottie listened, her heart aching for the man before her. She could see the toll those years had taken on him, the weariness that lingered beneath the surface. "But you're not that person anymore, Alex. You've grown, changed. Found new purpose."

He nodded, a faint smile tugging at his lips. "I have. And so much of that is because of you, Lottie. You've shown me that there's more to life than the spotlight. That true happiness comes from the quiet moments, the simple joys."

She smiled, her eyes shining with love and understanding. "And you've shown me the power of second chances, of embracing change and taking risks. Together, we've created something beautiful."

Alex's gaze locked with hers, the intensity of his emotions nearly overwhelming. "I don't want to lose this, Lottie. What we have, it's... it's everything."

Lottie leaned in, her forehead resting against his. "You won't lose me, Alex. No matter what you decide, I'm here. I believe in you, in us."

Alex's heart raced as Lottie's words washed over him, her unwavering support a beacon in the darkness of his doubts. He drew in a deep breath, the scent of her perfume mingling with the faint aroma of aged vinyl that permeated the room. In her eyes, he saw a reflection of the man he had become, the man she had helped him discover beneath the layers of his rock star persona.

"Lottie," he whispered, his voice rough with emotion. "You've given me something I never thought I'd find again. A reason to believe in myself, to trust in the power of connection."

She smiled, her fingers tracing the lines of his face with a tenderness that made his heart ache. "And you've given me the courage to embrace my own dreams, to step out of my comfort zone and into a world of possibility."

Alex's mind wandered to the countless nights they had spent together, exploring the depths of their passion and the intricacies of their souls. The way her body fit so perfectly against his, the way her laughter filled the spaces between his heartbeats. He knew, with a certainty that settled deep in his bones, that he couldn't bear to lose the magic they had found together.

"I choose you, Lottie," he said, his voice steady and sure. "I choose us, and the life we've begun to build. The fame, the fortune, it all pales in comparison to the love I feel for you."

Lottie's eyes widened, her breath catching in her throat as the weight of his words sank in. "Alex, are you sure? I don't want you to have any regrets, to wonder what might have been."

He shook his head, a smile spreading across his face. "The only regret I could ever have would be letting you go. You're my future, Lottie. My heart, my home."

As he drew her into his arms, their lips meeting in a kiss that spoke of passion, promise, and the unbreakable bond they shared, Alex knew that he had made the right choice. The path ahead might be uncertain, but with Lottie by his side, he was ready to face whatever challenges lay in store. Together, they would write a new chapter in their love story, one filled with music, laughter, and the enduring power of second chances.

As their lips parted, a sigh of contentment escaped Lottie's mouth. The warmth of her breath mingled with the scent of aged paper and vinyl records, a reminder of the sanctuary they had found in The Velvet Room. Alex's fingers gently traced the curve of her jaw, his touch sending shivers down her spine.

He leaned in, whispering in her ear, "I want you, Lottie. Here. Now."

Her heart raced at the urgency in his voice. She nodded, her breath hitching as she took his hand and led him towards the secluded corner of the store, where a plush velvet couch beckoned. The soft glow of the antique lamps cast a romantic haze, illuminating the space with an intimate ambiance.

They sank into the cushions, their bodies pressed together, limbs entwining as their kisses deepened. Alex's hands roamed over her curves, savoring the feel of her beneath his fingertips. Lottie's own hands explored the contours of his muscular chest, the roughness of his jeans a tantalizing contrast to the softness of his shirt.

Their connection was electric, a tangible force that seemed to pulse through the air around them. As they slipped further into the throes of passion, the outside world faded away, leaving only the two of them and the rhythm of their hearts beating in sync.

With a gentle touch, Alex guided Lottie onto her back, his body hovering above hers as he peppered her neck with soft kisses. She arched beneath him, her fingers tangling in his hair, lost in the sensation of his lips on her skin.

Clothes were shed slowly, deliberately, each article revealing more of the beauty they held so dear. The sounds of their breathing melded with the distant strains of an old vinyl record playing softly in the background, creating a symphony of love and desire.

As their bodies merged, Alex paused, looking deep into Lottie's eyes. He saw the love, the trust, the unspoken promise that bound them together. With a tender smile, he whispered, "I love you, Lottie. More than words can say."

Tears welled in her eyes as she replied, "I love you too, Alex. Now and always."

sixteen

. . .

The fading sunlight streamed through the dusty windows of **The Velvet Room**, casting long shadows across the worn wooden floors. Lottie's fingers traced the grooves of a vintage record sleeve as she waited for Alex, her heart fluttering with nervous anticipation.

The bell above the door chimed, and there he was - all tousled hair and piercing blue eyes. Lottie's breath caught in her throat. Even after all this time, Alex's presence still made her pulse race.

"Hey," he said, his deep voice sending a shiver down her spine.

"Hi," Lotte replied softly, tucking a strand of black hair behind her ear. "Thanks for coming."

Alex nodded, his gaze roaming over the shelves of records. "This place brings back memories."

Lottie watched him, wondering what ghosts of his past were swirling through his mind. She cleared her throat. "So, I've been thinking about how we can save the venue."

Alex's eyes snapped back to her, suddenly alert. "Let's hear it."

Lottie took a deep breath, mustering her courage. "What if we organized a series of intimate acoustic shows? Showcase both big names and up-and-comers. Generate some buzz."

A slow smile spread across Alex's face, crinkling the corners of his eyes. "I like the way you think, Charlotte Madden."

Her cheeks flushed at the use of her full name. "Really? You don't think it's too ambitious?"

Alex shook his head, his expression softening. "It's perfect. Intimate shows are what music is all about - that raw connection between artist and audience."

Lottie nodded eagerly, her excitement building. "Exactly! We could create something really special here."

As they dove into planning, tossing ideas back and forth, Lottie felt a spark ignite between them. Their shared passion for music bridged the gap of years and experience, creating a connection that left her breathless.

She watched Alex gesticulate as he described his vision, marveling at how animated he became when talking about music. In these moments, she could see glimpses of the rock star he once was, passion burning bright beneath his guarded exterior.

What would it be like to ignite that passion in other ways? The unbidden thought sent heat rushing to her cheeks. Lottie pushed it aside, forcing herself to focus on the task at hand.

This was about saving the venue, she reminded herself sternly. Nothing more. But as Alex's eyes met hers, filled with warmth and possibility, Lottie couldn't help but wonder if they might be on the verge of creating something far more profound than just a concert series.

Lottie tucked a strand of black hair behind her ear, her mind racing with possibilities. "I think I know just where to start," she said, her voice soft but filled with determination. "There's this indie folk band, 'Whispered Echoes,' that plays at The Rusty Nail every Thursday.

They've got a sound that would be perfect for what we're envisioning."

Alex leaned forward, intrigued. "Tell me more."

"Their lead singer, Mia, has this hauntingly beautiful voice that could make a stone weep," Lottie explained, her eyes lighting up. "I've chatted with her a few times at **The Velvet Room**. I think she'd be thrilled at the opportunity to perform in a more intimate setting."

As she spoke, Lottie's mind wandered to the endless shelves of vinyl at the record store, the familiar scent of aged paper and the soft crackle of a needle hitting grooves. It was her sanctuary, a place where she felt most herself. Now, she was bringing that passion here, to this venue that held so much potential.

Alex nodded, a small smile playing at the corners of his mouth. "Sounds promising. Any other local talents you've got up your sleeve?"

Lottie felt a surge of confidence. "Oh, I've got a whole list. There's 'The Midnight Troubadours,' a jazz quartet that would add some nice variety. And 'Neon Heartache,' a synth-pop duo that's been gaining traction on the local scene."

As she rattled off names and descriptions, Alex's eyes never left her face. The intensity of his gaze made her stomach flutter, a mix of nerves and something else she couldn't quite name.

"You're full of surprises, Charlotte Madden," Alex said, his deep voice sending a shiver down her spine. "I think we've got the makings of a solid lineup here."

Lottie blushed, both pleased and flustered by his praise. "Thanks. I just hope they'll all be interested in participating."

"With you championing the cause? How could they resist?" Alex's words were tinged with warmth that made Lottie's heart skip a beat.

She cleared her throat, trying to regain her composure. "So, um, what about promotion? We need to get the word out somehow."

Lottie's fingers itched to create, her mind already swirling with vibrant colors and bold designs. "I'll take charge of the flyers and posters," she said, her voice soft but determined. "I want to capture the essence of what we're doing here."

Alex's eyebrows rose, a flicker of intrigue crossing his face. "You design, too? Is there anything you can't do?"

A nervous laugh escaped her lips. "Oh, plenty. But this... this I can do." She closed her eyes for a moment, envisioning the perfect blend of vintage charm and modern edge. "I'm thinking rich, warm tones with pops of neon. A mix of old and new, just like our partnership."

Alex leaned in, his proximity sending a jolt through her system. "I like the sound of that. Make sure to include both our names prominently. We're in this together, after all."

Lottie's heart raced at his words. Together. It felt right, somehow.

"Speaking of making a splash," Alex continued, his blue eyes gleaming with an idea, "what do you think about hosting a press conference?"

Lottie blinked, caught off guard. "A press conference? Isn't that a bit... much?"

Alex chuckled, the sound low and rich. "Trust me, in this industry, there's no such thing as 'too much.' We invite local journalists, music insiders, maybe even some of your musician friends. Generate some buzz, you know?"

Lottie bit her lip, uncertainty gnawing at her. "I don't know, Alex. The spotlight's not really my thing."

He reached out, his calloused fingers brushing her arm. "Hey, I'll be right there with you. We're a team now, remember?"

The warmth of his touch lingered, and Lottie found herself nodding. "Okay. Let's do it."

As they delved into the details, Lottie couldn't help but marvel at the strange turns life could take. Here she was, planning events and press conferences with a former rock star. It was terrifying and exhilarating all at once, like standing on the edge of a cliff, ready to take flight.

Lottie's fingers trembled as she dialed the number, her heart a thunderous drum in her chest. The phone rang once, twice, before a cheerful voice answered.

"Stellar Events, this is Mona speaking!"

Lottie swallowed hard, her voice barely above a whisper. "Hi, I'm Charlotte Madden. I... I need help organizing some performances."

As Lottie stumbled through explaining their plans, her mind wandered. *Was she really doing this? The shy bookworm, planning music events?* It felt like wearing someone else's skin.

Meanwhile, across town, Alex lounged in his living room, phone in hand. The faded concert posters on the walls seemed to mock him, ghosts of a past life. He scrolled through his contacts, names he hadn't spoken in years.

"Hey, Dave," he said, his voice gruff from disuse. "It's Alex. Yeah, that Alex. Listen, I've got a proposition for you..."

One by one, Alex reached out to old friends and collaborators. Some calls were awkward, others filled with laughter and shared memories. With each conversation, he felt a spark of something he thought he'd lost - excitement.

"So, what do you say?" Alex asked, running a hand through his salt-and-pepper hair. "Want to be part of something new?"

As the sun dipped below the horizon, casting long shadows across **The Velvet Room**, Lottie and Alex's separate efforts wove together, creating the first threads of a tapestry neither could have imagined alone.

* * *

THE DIM LIGHT of **The Velvet Room** cast a warm glow over Lottie and Alex as they huddled around a makeshift planning board. Vinyl sleeves and concert flyers littered the floor, a chaotic mosaic of their shared passion.

"What about The Whisper Sisters for the opening night?" Lottie suggested, her voice soft but determined. She held up an indie folk album, its cover adorned with ethereal imagery.

Alex leaned in, his piercing blue eyes studying the sleeve. "Hmm, good choice. We could follow them with Jack Thunder's new blues project. Create a nice contrast."

Lottie nodded, a small smile playing on her lips. She marveled at how easily they fell into sync, two vastly different souls united by the language of music.

"We need something edgier for the second week," Alex mused, running a hand through his tousled hair. "Maybe that new punk outfit, Rage Against the Washing Machine?"

A burst of laughter escaped Lottie, surprising even herself. "That name is ridiculous," she giggled, "but their sound is incredible. Let's do it."

As they worked, Lottie couldn't help but steal glances at Alex. His face, lined with years of experience, lit up with each decision. She wondered about the stories behind those laugh lines, the triumphs and heartaches that had shaped him.

"Okay, sponsorships," Alex said, breaking her reverie. "Any ideas?"

Lottie bit her lip, thinking. "What about Local Brew? They've been supportive of the arts scene."

"Good thinking," Alex nodded. "I've got a contact at Sound Wave Equipment. They might be willing to provide some gear in exchange for promotion."

As they brainstormed, Lottie felt a warmth spreading through her chest. This wasn't just about saving the venue anymore. It was about creating something beautiful, something that could touch people's lives. And doing it with Alex... well, that was an unexpected bonus she was trying hard not to dwell on.

Lottie reached for her planner, its pages already dog-eared and filled with scribbled notes. "We should map out a timeline," she suggested, her voice soft but determined. "Make sure we're not missing anything crucial."

Alex nodded, leaning in closer. The scent of sandalwood and leather enveloped her, making her heart skip. "Good idea. Let's break it down week by week."

They huddled over the planner, their heads nearly touching. Lottie's hand trembled slightly as she wrote, hyperaware of Alex's proximity.

"First things first," Alex said, his deep voice resonating through her. "We need to secure the venue dates."

Lottie jotted it down, her neat handwriting a stark contrast to the chaos of emotions swirling inside her. "Right. Then we should start reaching out to the artists we want to feature."

As they worked through the timeline, Lottie found herself marveling at Alex's attention to detail. For someone who had once commanded stadium-sized crowds, he seemed genuinely invested in every aspect of these intimate shows.

"What about dividing up the workload?" Lotte asked, finally voicing the question that had been nagging at her. "There's so much to do."

Alex leaned back, his blue eyes meeting hers. "Well, you've got a knack for promotion. Why don't you take charge of marketing? I can handle the artistic side, coordinating with the performers."

Lottie nodded, a mix of excitement and nervousness

bubbling up inside her. "I'd like that," she said softly, wondering if she was up to the task.

As they finished outlining their plan, Alex reached for two glasses and a bottle of aged whiskey tucked away in a corner of the venue's office. Lottie watched as he poured the amber liquid, his strong hands steady and sure.

"I think we've earned this," Alex said, handing her a glass. His fingers brushed hers, sending a jolt through her body.

Lottie raised her glass, the crystal catching the dim light. "To new beginnings," she offered, her voice barely above a whisper.

"And to facing challenges head-on," Alex added, his eyes twinkling with a mix of determination and something else Lottie couldn't quite place.

They clinked glasses, the sound echoing in the quiet room. Lottie took a sip, the whiskey burning a path down her throat. She coughed slightly, unused to the strong liquor.

Alex chuckled, a deep, rich sound that made her stomach flutter. "Too strong?"

"No, it's... it's good," Lottie managed, taking another small sip. This time, she savored the complex flavors, letting them linger on her tongue. "I can see why you like it."

"It grows on you," Alex said, his voice soft. "Like many things in life."

Lottie felt a blush creeping up her neck. Was he talking about the whiskey, or something else entirely?

"We should get started," she said quickly, setting down her glass. "There's so much to do."

Alex nodded, finishing his drink in one smooth motion. "You're right. Time to put our plan into action."

As they gathered their things, Lottie couldn't help but feel a surge of excitement mixed with trepidation. *What had she gotten herself into? And why did it feel so thrilling?*

Lottie fumbled with her messenger bag, her fingers clumsy as she tried to stuff her notebook inside. Alex's presence loomed large, his cologne a heady mix of sandalwood and something distinctly masculine. She inhaled deeply, trying to steady her nerves.

"You okay there?" Alex asked, his voice laced with concern.

"Fine," Lottie squeaked, then cleared her throat. "Just... a lot on my mind."

Alex's hand brushed her arm, sending shivers down her spine. "We've got this, Lottie. Together."

She looked up, meeting his piercing blue eyes. Time seemed to stand still, the air crackling with unspoken tension. Lottie's heart raced, her mind a whirlwind of conflicting emotions.

"I know," she finally managed, her voice barely audible. "It's just... overwhelming sometimes."

Alex's expression softened. "Trust me, I get it. But that's why we make a good team. You've got the fresh perspective, and I've got the battle scars."

Lottie couldn't help but laugh. "Battle scars? Is that what we're calling your rockstar days now?"

"Hey, those mosh pits were brutal," Alex retorted, a grin playing at the corners of his mouth.

As they gathered the last of their belongings, Lottie felt a newfound sense of purpose settling over her. This crazy plan might just work, she thought. And even if it didn't, the journey itself promised to be one hell of a ride.

They moved towards the door, Alex's hand hovering near the small of her back, not quite touching but close enough to make her pulse quicken. As they stepped out into the cool night air, their eyes met once more.

seventeen

. . .

They moved through the venue like a well-oiled machine, checking and double-checking every detail. Alex fiddled with the sound system, his experienced hands coaxing crystal-clear notes from the speakers. Lottie adjusted the lighting, creating a warm, inviting ambiance that seemed to make the very air shimmer with possibility.

As they worked, Lottie couldn't help but steal glances at Alex. The way he moved with such confidence, the intensity in his eyes as he focused on each task - it was intoxicating. She found herself wondering what it would be like to be the sole focus of that intense gaze, to feel those strong hands on her...

"Lottie?" Alex's voice snapped her out of her reverie. "Everything okay?"

She blushed, grateful for the dim lighting. "Yeah, just... lost in thought. This is really happening, isn't it?"

Alex's smile was warm, genuine. "It sure is. And there's no one I'd rather do this with than you."

The words hung in the air between them, heavy with unspoken meaning. Lottie's heart raced as she wondered if he meant more than just the music events. But before she could respond, Alex's phone buzzed with incoming messages.

"They're in," he announced, his eyes lighting up with excitement. "Every single one of them."

Lottie's face split into a wide grin, her earlier thoughts momentarily forgotten in the rush of success. "That's amazing! We're really doing this, Alex."

As they celebrated their small victory, Lottie couldn't shake the feeling that they were on the cusp of something much bigger than just a series of concerts. Something that could change both their lives forever.

THE BACKSTAGE AREA buzzed with nervous energy as Lottie and Alex greeted the performers. Lottie's hands trembled slightly as she handed out water bottles and adjusted microphones, her eyes darting to Alex every few seconds.

"You're doing great," he murmured, his hand briefly touching the small of her back. The warmth of his touch sent shivers down her spine.

"Thanks," she whispered back, fighting the urge to lean into him. "I just hope everything goes smoothly."

A wry chuckle escaped Alex's lips. "In live music? Never. But that's half the fun."

As if on cue, one of the guitarists approached them, panic evident in his eyes. "My string just snapped. Do you have a spare?"

"I've got you covered," Alex replied smoothly, reaching into a nearby case. Lottie marveled at his calm demeanor, a stark contrast to the jittery butterflies in her stomach.

The venue doors creaked open, and the first trickle of attendees began to filter in. Lottie took a deep breath, steeling herself.

"Showtime," Alex winked, gently nudging her towards the growing crowd.

As they mingled with the guests, Lottie found herself relaxing into the role of hostess. She smiled, shook hands, and made small talk, all while acutely aware of Alex's presence nearby.

"This place is amazing," one attendee gushed. "How long have you two been running it?"

Lottie hesitated, unsure how to explain their unique situation. "Oh, we're actually just getting started. It's a bit of a long story..."

She trailed off, catching Alex's eye across the room. He gave her a reassuring nod, and suddenly, the weight of their shared secret felt a little lighter.

* * *

THE FIRST ARTIST took the stage, a young woman with a guitar and a voice like honey. As she strummed the opening chords, the venue crackled with electric anticipation. Lottie felt goosebumps rise on her arms, her breath catching in her throat.

"We did it," Alex murmured beside her, his voice barely audible over the music. Lottie turned to him, her eyes shining with unshed tears of joy.

"I can't believe this is real," she whispered back, her heart swelling with pride.

As the night progressed, Lottie and Alex fell into an easy rhythm. They moved through the venue like a well-oiled machine, anticipating each other's needs without a word.

When the sound system crackled during the third set, Alex was already on it, deftly adjusting knobs and wires. Lottie smoothly stepped in to distract the audience, sharing an anecdote about the venue's history that had them chuckling.

"Nice save," Alex murmured as he rejoined her, his fingers brushing her arm. The touch sent a jolt through Lottie, reminding her of the spark between them that she was trying desperately to ignore.

A last-minute cancellation threatened to derail the schedule, but Lottie quickly rearranged the lineup, her grandmother's old planner proving invaluable. Alex handled the nervous replacement act with practiced ease, his calm demeanor soothing their jitters.

As Lottie watched him work, she couldn't help but marvel at the contrast between the Alex she knew and the rock legend he once was. This Alex, with his quiet competence and gentle guidance, seemed a world away from the wild frontman of Hollow Reign.

"We make a good team," she found herself saying, surprising even herself with the admission.

Alex's eyes crinkled at the corners as he smiled. "That we do, Lottie. That we do."

IN A QUIET MOMENT BETWEEN SETS,

Lottie found herself pulled into a secluded corner backstage. Alex's strong arms enveloped her, his scent - a mix of sandalwood and something uniquely him - enveloping her senses.

"You're incredible," he whispered, his lips brushing her ear. "The way you handled that crowd..."

Lottie felt her cheeks flush. "I learned from the best," she murmured, tilting her face up to his.

Their lips met in a kiss that was equal parts tender and passionate. Lottie's heart raced, her body melting into his as if they were made to fit together.

"We should get back," she said reluctantly, even as her fingers tangled in his salt-and-pepper locks.

Alex nodded, stealing one more quick kiss. "You're right. But later..."

His unfinished promise hung in the air, electric with possibility.

As they parted, Lottie caught sight of herself in a dusty mirror. Her eyes were bright, her cheeks flushed. She barely recognized the confident woman staring back at her.

The final act took the stage, their haunting melody filling the venue. Lottie and Alex stood side by side, fingers intertwined.

"We did it," Lottie whispered, awe in her voice.

Alex squeezed her hand. "No, love. You did it. I just helped a little."

As the last notes faded, the crowd erupted into thunderous applause. Alex tugged Lottie gently towards the stage.

"Ready?" he asked, his blue eyes twinkling.

Lottie took a deep breath and nodded. Together, they stepped into the spotlight.

THE APPLAUSE slowly died down as Lottie and Alex made their way through the dispersing crowd. A kaleidoscope of emotions swirled within Lottie - pride, exhaustion, exhilaration.

"That was bloody brilliant!" A man with a press badge approached them, his eyes gleaming. "You've really breathed new life into this place."

Lottie smiled shyly. "Thank you, we-"

"It's all thanks to Lottie here," Alex interjected, his hand warm on the small of her back. "She's the visionary behind it all."

The reporter scribbled furiously in his notebook. "And will there be more events like this?"

"Absolutely," Lottie replied, surprised by the confidence in her own voice. "We're just getting started."

As they navigated through a sea of congratulations and handshakes, Lottie caught snippets of excited chatter.

"Best show I've seen in years!"

"Can't wait for the next one!"

"Who knew this old place could rock like that?"

Alex leaned in close, his breath tickling her ear. "Hear that? You've given them something to talk about."

Lottie's heart swelled. She had done it. She had honored her grandmother's legacy while creating something uniquely her own.

"Let's slip away," Alex murmured, his fingers intertwining with hers. "I think we deserve a private celebration."

Lottie nodded, suddenly aware of how desperately she craved a moment alone with him. They made their way to the small office tucked away backstage, closing the door on the world outside.

* * *

THE OFFICE, once a cluttered mess, now felt like a sanctuary. Lottie sank into the worn leather couch, her body finally registering the exhaustion of the day. Alex popped open a bottle of champagne, the cork hitting the ceiling with a satisfying thunk.

"To us," he said, handing her a glass. "And to the magic we've created."

Lottie took a sip, the bubbles dancing on her tongue. "I can't believe we actually pulled it off."

Alex settled beside her, his arm draping around her shoulders. "Did you doubt we would?"

"Honestly? A little," Lottie admitted, nestling into his warmth. "It all seemed so... impossible at first."

"But look at what you've accomplished," Alex murmured, his fingers tracing lazy circles on her arm. "You've turned this place into something extraordinary."

Lottie closed her eyes, letting the events of the night wash over her. The music, the energy, the palpable excitement in the air. It was intoxicating.

"We did it together," she said softly. "I couldn't have done any of this without you."

Alex's lips brushed against her temple. "You underestimate yourself, love. But I'm glad I could be part of it."

They lapsed into a comfortable silence, the muffled sounds of the crowd outside slowly fading away. Lottie felt herself drifting, caught between exhaustion and elation.

"What are you thinking about?" Alex asked, his voice low and intimate.

Lottie opened her eyes, meeting his gaze. "The future. Where we go from here."

eighteen

. . .

The sleek black car purred to a stop, its tinted windows reflecting the neon signs of the music venue. Alex's breath caught in his throat as the front door swung open.

Delilah Blackwood emerged like a vision from the past, her platinum blonde hair catching the evening breeze. She stood tall, her presence electric, commanding attention without uttering a word.

Alex's feet refused to move, rooted to the spot as if the weight of their shared history had suddenly materialized. His eyes widened, a mix of surprise and apprehension clouding his blue gaze.

"Delilah," he whispered, the name both familiar and foreign on his tongue.

She turned, green eyes locking onto him with laser-like precision. A knowing smile played on her lips, igniting memories Alex had long tried to bury.

His heart raced, thoughts tumbling over each other. *Why is she here? After all this time?*

"Alex," Delilah's voice carried across the space between them, low and melodic. "It's been too long."

He swallowed hard, fighting the urge to run or embrace her—he wasn't sure which. "What are you doing here?"

She laughed, the sound both alluring and unsettling. "Can't an old friend drop by?"

Friend. The word hung in the air, laden with unspoken truths and half-forgotten promises.

Alex's fingers twitched, muscle memory recalling the feel of guitar strings, of her skin. He forced them still. "It's been years, Lila."

The old nickname slipped out before he could stop it. Delilah's eyes flashed with something—triumph? Regret? It was gone too quickly to decipher.

"Years fade, darling," she said, taking a step closer. "But some things never change."

The scent of her perfume hit him, a heady mix of jasmine and danger. Alex's mind reeled, caught between the pull of the past and the tentative hope of his present.

"Everything's changed," he managed, his voice rougher than he intended.

Delilah's smile widened, a predator-sensing weakness. "Has it really, Alex? Have you?"

* * *

LOTTIE'S ATTENTION snapped away from her conversation, drawn by an electric change in the air. She turned, her black hair swinging softly, to see a striking blonde woman standing at the entrance. The newcomer's presence seemed to suck all the oxygen from the room.

Lottie's breath caught. "Excuse me," she murmured to the artist, her eyes never leaving the scene unfolding before her.

The blonde's emerald gaze locked onto Alex, a knowing smile playing on her crimson lips. Each step she took towards him echoed through the venue, her heels clicking a staccato rhythm against the worn wooden floor.

Click. Click. Click.

Lottie's heart matched the tempo, quickening with each step the woman took. She watched, transfixed, as Alex's face cycled through a kaleidoscope of emotions—surprise, fear, longing, regret.

Who is she? Lottie wondered, her fingers unconsciously twisting the vintage bracelet on her wrist. The way Alex looked at her... it was like seeing a ghost.

The air crackled with unspoken history, heavy with the weight of shared secrets. Lottie felt like an intruder, witnessing something intimate and raw. Yet she couldn't look away, couldn't quell the rising tide of jealousy and curiosity threatening to overwhelm her.

As the distance between Alex and the mysterious woman closed, Lottie found herself taking a hesitant step forward, drawn into their orbit like a moth to a flame.

* * *

ALEX'S CHEST TIGHTENED, each breath a struggle as memories assaulted him. Delilah's laugh, low and throaty, echoed in his mind. Flashes of tangled sheets, heated arguments, and tear-stained goodbyes flickered through his consciousness like a broken film reel.

"Shit," he muttered under his breath, running a hand through his salt-and-pepper locks. The familiar scent of Delilah's perfume—jasmine and spice—wafted towards him, threatening to drown him in nostalgia.

Lottie approached, her soft footsteps barely audible over the pounding of his heart. "Alex?" she whispered, her warm brown eyes filled with concern. "Is everything okay?"

He turned to her, grateful for the anchor she provided. "Lottie, I—" he started, but the words caught in his throat.

Her gaze flickered between him and Delilah, curiosity and apprehension warring on her face. "Do you know her?"

Alex swallowed hard, his Adam's apple bobbing. "Yeah," he managed, his voice rough. "From... before."

Lottie's hand found his arm, a gentle touch that sent a jolt through him. "She seems to know you pretty well," she observed, a hint of something—jealousy?—coloring her tone.

"It's complicated," Alex sighed, feeling the weight of his past pressing down on him. He wanted to explain, to reassure Lottie, but Delilah was getting closer, her green eyes never leaving his face.

"Isn't it always?" Lottie murmured, her fingers tightening slightly on his arm.

Delilah's voice, low and melodic, cut through the tension like a velvet knife. "Alex, darling. It's been far too long."

Her words hung in the air, heavy with unspoken history. Alex felt a shiver run down his spine, memories of late-night studio sessions and passionate embraces threatening to overwhelm him.

"Delilah," he managed, his voice hoarse. "I didn't expect to see you here."

She laughed, the sound both familiar and foreign. "Oh, you know me. I love a good surprise." Her gaze flicked to Lottie, a predatory glint in her eyes. "And who's this charming young thing?"

Alex's mind raced, torn between his tumultuous past with Delilah and the promise of something new with Lottie. He opened his mouth, then closed it, words failing him.

Lottie stepped forward, her chin lifted in subtle defiance. "I'm Charlotte Madden. I own this venue."

"Ah, the infamous inheritance," Delilah purred. "How... quaint."

Alex felt the urge to defend Lottie, but found himself paralyzed. His eyes darted between the two women – Delilah, all sleek confidence and dangerous allure, and Lottie, with her quiet strength and gentle spirit.

"What brings you here, Lila?" he asked, falling back on her old nickname without thinking.

Delilah's smile widened, a cat toying with its prey. "Oh, you know. Old times, new opportunities. The usual." She leaned in, her perfume enveloping him. "We have so much to catch up on, Alex. Remember that night in Tokyo?"

Alex's breath caught. Of course he remembered. The sake, the thunderstorm, the way she'd looked in the neon lights. He shook his head, trying to clear it. "That was a long time ago," he said, his voice rough.

Lottie shifted beside him, and he felt a pang of guilt. He turned to her, seeing the questions in her eyes. "Lottie, I—"

But before he could finish, Delilah's hand was on his arm, her touch electric. "Come now, Alex. The past is never really past, is it? Not for us."

Lottie's intuition flared, a warning bell clanging in her mind. She saw the conflict in Alex's eyes, the way his body tensed at Delilah's touch. Without thinking, she took a step closer to him, her hand reaching out to gently rest on his other arm.

The warmth of Lottie's touch grounded Alex, pulling him back from the swirling vortex of memories Delilah had stirred up. He glanced down at Lottie's hand, then up to her face, seeing the silent support in her warm brown eyes. A surge of gratitude washed over him, mingled with a newfound resolve.

"You're right, Lottie's here now," Alex said, his voice steadier. "And we've got a venue to run."

Delilah's gaze flickered to Lottie's hand on Alex's arm, her green eyes narrowing almost imperceptibly. For a split second, something dark and unreadable flashed across her face – jealousy? Anger? Calculation? – before her usual mask of composure slipped back into place.

"How sweet," Delilah murmured, her tone hovering between genuine and mocking. "I do so love to see new... partnerships forming."

Lottie felt a chill run down her spine at Delilah's words, but she kept her hand firmly on Alex's arm, her thumb tracing small, comforting circles. She wouldn't be intimidated, not in her own venue, not when Alex needed her strength.

Alex's jaw clenched, his blue eyes stormy with conflict. He ran a hand through his salt-and-pepper hair, a gesture Lottie had come to recognize as a sign of his internal struggle.

"Delilah," he said, his voice low and gravelly. "That was a long time ago."

Lottie's heart raced, her mind conjuring images of Alex and Delilah together. She fought to push them away, focusing instead on the warmth of Alex's arm beneath her hand.

"Not so long ago that you've forgotten, I hope," Delilah purred, taking a step closer.

Lottie felt Alex tense beside her. She squeezed his arm gently, a reminder of her presence, of their connection.

"Look," Lottie said, surprising herself with the strength in her voice. "Whatever happened between you two in the past, it's just that - the past. Alex is with me now."

Delilah's eyebrows raised, amusement dancing in her green eyes. "Is that so?"

Alex cleared his throat, his gaze flickering between the two women. "Lottie's right," he said, his voice rough with emotion. "Things have changed, Delilah. I've changed."

Lottie's heart swelled at his words, but she couldn't ignore the flicker of pain that crossed Delilah's face. For a moment, the older woman's mask slipped, revealing a vulnerability that made Lottie's chest ache with an unexpected empathy.

"I see," Delilah said softly, composing herself. "Well, isn't this interesting?"

Delilah's eyes narrowed slightly, her gaze flickering between Alex and Lottie. The air crackled with tension, like the moment before lightning strikes. Lottie felt her pulse quicken, her fingers still resting on Alex's arm.

"Well, my dear," Delilah said, her voice a low purr. She gave a slight nod, acknowledging Lottie's words. "You certainly have spirit. I can see why Alex is... intrigued."

There was a glimmer in Delilah's eyes, a flash of something dangerous and alluring. Lottie felt a chill run down her spine. This woman was like a beautiful, poisonous flower - captivating and deadly.

Alex shifted beside her, his muscles tense. "Delilah, what are you doing here?" he asked, his voice strained.

Delilah's lips curved into a knowing smile. "Oh, Alex. You know I can never stay away for long. We have... unfinished business."

Lottie's mind raced. Unfinished business? What did that mean? She felt like she was standing on the edge of a precipice, about to tumble into a world she didn't understand.

"Whatever it is," Lottie said, surprised by the steadiness in her voice, "it can wait. We're in the middle of something here."

Delilah's eyebrow arched, that challenging glimmer intensifying in her gaze. "Are we? How... inconvenient."

Lottie felt the weight of unspoken history pressing down on them. *What had happened between Alex and this woman? And why did she feel so threatened by her presence?*

"We're still married, love," Delilah spat out watching the oxygen sucked out of the room.

nineteen

. . .

The air backstage crackled with tension, thick as guitar strings about to snap. Alex's fingers twitched, muscle memory seeking the familiar weight of an instrument that wasn't there.

Delilah materialized from the shadows, her platinum hair a beacon in the dim light. Her green eyes locked onto Alex, filled with a storm of emotions he couldn't quite decipher.

Lottie left the room, giving Alex and Delilah a moment to talk ... giving herself time to think about what the fuck was going on.

. . .

"WE NEED TO TALK," Delilah said, her voice low and hypnotic.

Alex's heart hammered against his ribs. "Lila, I—"

"No," she cut him off, raising a perfectly manicured hand. "It's time for you to listen."

He swallowed hard, acutely aware of the sweat beading on his forehead. Lila took a step closer, her presence overwhelming in the confined space.

"You have a choice to make, Alex," she said, her tone wavering slightly. "Your past or your future. Me or her."

The ultimatum hung in the air between them, heavy as a discordant chord. Alex's mind raced, memories of sold-out stadiums and whiskey-soaked nights clashing with quiet evenings spent listening to vinyl with Lottie.

"I don't—" he began, but the words died in his throat.

Lila's eyes narrowed. "Don't tell me you're actually considering that girl. She can't give you what I can, what we have."

Alex's gaze darted to the backstage entrance, half-expecting Lottie to walk in at any moment. The thought filled him with equal parts dread and longing.

"It's not that simple," he managed, running a hand through his salt-and-pepper hair.

"Isn't it?" Lila challenged, her voice rising. "You're Alex King. You're meant for more than small-town obscurity and dusty record shops."

The words stung, hitting too close to his own doubts. But as he opened his mouth to respond, an image of Lottie's warm brown eyes flashed in his mind, grounding him.

"I've changed, Lila," he said softly, surprised by the steadiness in his voice. "Maybe I want something different now."

Lila's expression flickered, a mix of disbelief and something that might have been hurt. "You can't mean that."

Alex's heart raced as he searched for the right words, torn between the allure of his past and the promise of his future.

"Remember Paris?" Lila's voice softened, a hint of vulnerability creeping in. "The way we danced on the Pont des Arts at midnight?"

Alex closed his eyes, the image vivid in his mind. "I remember," he murmured, his deep voice barely audible.

But with the sweet memory came the bitter aftertaste – the fights, the betrayals, the endless cycle of reconciliation and heartbreak. His fingers twitched, muscle memory reaching for a guitar that wasn't there.

"It wasn't all good times, Lila," he said, opening his eyes to meet her gaze. "We can't go back. I want to sign those divorce papers now."

Delilah laughed wickedly, "Oh, *now* you want to sign the papers? When all this time you've been hanging onto hope?"

Alex swallowed the bile that was surfacing in his throat. "Yeah, I was … but now I know it's over between us. You living a thousand miles away for the past five years proved that to me. *You're* the one who walked out on me, love. *You're* the one who I found fucking two guys in our bed —that was *you* —not *me*."

Delilah gazed down at the ground and dug her heel into the concrete. "I'm sorry for that Alex, I really am. But time away from you only proved how much I want us back. I still love you."

"That's just it, Delilah, I don't love you," Alex quickly replied. "I don't."

"But I still love you," Delilah cried.

Alex shook his head, no. "You want that lifestyle back—you've always been addicted to it—more so than me. You read all the noise that *Hollow Reign* is back to making music and you want to be that glorified groupie again. But I don't want that anymore—get it through your fucking head. I'm done."

Before Lila could respond, the backstage door creaked open. Alex's heart leapt to his throat as Lottie stepped in, her black hair slightly disheveled, eyes wide as she took in the scene before her.

"Oh," Lottie breathed, her soft voice carrying in the sudden silence. "I'm sorry, I didn't mean to interrupt."

Alex watched as understanding dawned in Lottie's warm brown eyes. Without a word, she moved closer to him, her presence a balm to his frayed nerves. He felt the urge to reach for her hand but held back, acutely aware of Delilah's piercing gaze.

"You're not interrupting," Alex said, his voice steadier now. "We were just..."

He trailed off, unsure how to explain the situation. Lottie's quiet strength beside him was a stark contrast to the tumultuous emotions Delilah stirred. In that moment, the choice before him became startlingly clear.

Alex's eyes locked with Lottie's, and in her gaze, he found an anchor. The love and understanding radiating from her warm brown eyes washed over him like a soothing melody, drowning out the cacophony of his past. A glimmer of hope sparked in his chest, cutting through the fog of uncertainty.

"Lottie," he breathed, her name a prayer on his lips.

She didn't speak, but her eyes said everything. The slight tilt of her head, the soft curve of her lips – it was all the reassurance he needed. Alex took a deep breath, his shoulders straightening as he found his resolve.

Delilah's eyes narrowed, flicking between Alex and Lottie like a metronome counting out a tense rhythm. Her perfectly manicured nails dug into her palms, leaving crescent-shaped indents. The air crackled with unspoken tension.

"I see," Delilah said, her melodic voice tight with barely contained emotion. "So this is how it's going to be?"

A flicker of doubt crossed her face, a momentary crack in her confident facade. But as quickly as it appeared, it vanished, replaced by steely determination. Delilah lifted her chin, green eyes flashing with resolve.

"Remember what I said, Alex," she continued, her words a velvet-wrapped ultimatum. "The choice is yours, but make it wisely. Some doors, once closed, can never be reopened."

Alex's throat tightened, his heart pounding like a bass drum in his chest. He swallowed hard, tasting the bitterness of regret and the sweetness of new beginnings. His voice, once able to command stadiums, now trembled slightly as he spoke.

"Delilah, I..." he paused, searching for the right words. "...want a divorce. I'll see my lawyer and draw up new divorce papers. I no longer want to give you what you wanted before. And besides, you signed a prenup, you really deserve nothing."

He glanced at Lottie, drawing strength from her presence. Her vintage-inspired dress, so out of place in this backstage chaos, reminded him of vinyl records and quiet nights. Of peace.

"My heart," Alex continued, his words filled with a mix of determination and vulnerability, "it belongs here now. With Lottie. With the future, we're building together."

Lottie's breath caught in her throat, her heart swelling with relief and joy. She reached out, her delicate fingers intertwining with Alex's calloused ones. The contrast felt right, like a perfect harmony of rough and smooth.

As she squeezed his hand reassuringly, Lottie thought of the dusty shelves of **The Velvet Room**, of the stories hidden in each groove of those old records. She and Alex were writing their own story now, one track at a time.

In that moment, as their eyes met once more, they both knew. This was the right choice. This was their song, and it was only just beginning.

Delilah's piercing green eyes, once aflame with determination, now dimmed. Her shoulders sagged, the weight of Alex's decision visibly crushing her carefully constructed facade. A flicker of sadness passed through her gaze, like a shadow across a stage.

She nodded slowly, her platinum blonde hair catching the harsh backstage lighting. "I understand," she whispered, her melodic voice cracking slightly.

Without another word, Delilah turned on her heel, her dark clothing melting into the shadows as she silently exited the backstage area. The click of her stilettos faded, leaving Alex and Lottie alone in the sudden, deafening quiet.

Alex exhaled shakily, his chest tight with a mix of relief and lingering tension. He turned to Lottie, drinking in the sight of her warm brown eyes, finding solace in their depths.

Wordlessly, they fell into each other's arms, their bodies pressing together as if trying to meld into one. Alex buried his face in Lottie's black hair, inhaling the comforting scent of old books and vinyl.

"You chose me," Lottie murmured, her voice muffled against his chest. "You really chose me."

Alex pulled back slightly, cupping her face in his hands. "Always," he whispered, his blue eyes intense. "You're my new song, Lottie. My best one yet."

Lottie's heart soared at his words, feeling the truth of them resonate in her very bones. "And you're my unexpected verse," she replied, her literary mind conjuring the perfect metaphor. "The one that changes everything."

Their whispered words of love and reassurance blended into a harmonious melody, drowning out the distant hum of the waiting crowd beyond the curtain. In this moment, suspended in time, they were the only two people in the world.

As they slowly pulled apart, Alex and Lottie's eyes met in a knowing smile. The air between them crackled with newfound hope and determination, a silent promise of facing whatever lay ahead, together.

twenty

. . .

Six Months Later

The **Velvet Room** pulsed with electric energy, bodies pressed together like sardines in a tin. Lottie's palms were slick with sweat as she gripped the edge of the stage, her heart doing a frantic dance in her chest. The smell of beer and perfume mingled in the air, making her head spin.

She watched as a sea of faces turned expectantly toward the stage, hungry for a glimpse of Alex. *He's like a God up there! He has such a commanding stage presence!*

"You okay, hon?" A middle-aged woman with spiky hair nudged Lottie's arm. "You look like you're about to faint."

Lottie managed a weak smile. "I'm fine, thanks. Just...nervous."

The woman chuckled. "First time seeing *Hollow Reign* live? Don't worry, Alex may be older now but he still puts on one hell of a show."

If only she knew.

The roar of the crowd grew deafening as the house lights dimmed. This was it. Lottie's breath caught in her throat as she searched the darkened stage for any sign of Alex's tousled salt-and-pepper hair.

"Ladies and gentlemen," a disembodied voice boomed, "please welcome to the stage...Alex King!"

Time seemed to slow as Alex strode out, his presence magnetic. Even after all these months together, the sight of him still made Lottie's knees weak. Their eyes met across the sea of bodies, and for a heartbeat, it was just the two of them.

Then Alex turned to face the crowd, and Lottie's world narrowed to this moment, balanced on a knife's edge of anticipation.

The crowd's murmurs swelled into a cacophony of excited whispers and expectant chatter. Lottie caught snippets of conversation around her, each one stoking the fire of her anxiety.

"Is this a comeback tour?"

"God, he's still *so* hot."

"I heard he's been writing new material..."

Lottie's heart raced, her palms slick with sweat. She wiped them on her jeans, unable to tear her eyes away from Alex.

He stood there, larger than life, his piercing blue eyes scanning the audience. The stage lights caught the silver in his hair, making it shimmer like starlight. Alex took a deep breath, his chest expanding beneath his well-worn leather jacket. Lottie knew that look—he was steeling himself, gathering courage.

A hush fell over the crowd as Alex stepped up to the microphone. He gripped the stand, knuckles white, and for a moment, Lottie saw a flicker of vulnerability cross his face. It was gone in an instant, replaced by the cool confidence she'd fallen for.

"It's been a while," Alex's deep voice rumbled through the speakers, sending shivers down Lottie's spine. "I've got something important to say tonight."

Lottie's breath caught. This was it. The moment that would change everything.

Alex's eyes scanned the crowd, finally locking onto

Lottie's. The intensity of his gaze made her knees weak, and she gripped the edge of the stage for support.

"I've been running for a long time," Alex continued, his voice low and husky. "From fame, from my past, from myself. But sometimes, life has a way of catching up to you."

He paused, a wry smile tugging at the corner of his lips. Lottie's heart pounded so loudly she was sure everyone could hear it.

"I came here tonight to talk about new beginnings," Alex said, his fingers absently strumming the strings of his guitar. "But I realized there's something more important I need to say first."

Lottie held her breath, time seeming to stretch like taffy. The air crackled with electricity, every person in the room hanging on Alex's words.

"Charlotte Madden," he said, his voice breaking slightly on her name. "Lottie. You walked into my life like a whirlwind, turning everything upside down. And I've never been more grateful for anything in my life."

A collective gasp rippled through the audience. Lottie felt lightheaded, her vision tunneling until all she could see was Alex.

"I love you, Lottie," Alex declared, his words ringing out clear and true.

Lottie's mind reeled. *This can't be happening,* she thought. But the raw emotion in Alex's eyes told her it was real. All too real.

The crowd erupted into a cacophony of cheers and applause, the thunderous roar washing over Lottie like a tidal wave. Whistles pierced the air, and she caught snippets of excited chatter around her.

"Oh my god, did you hear that?"

"Alex King, in love? Who would've thought?"

"They look perfect together!"

Lottie stood frozen, her eyes wide with disbelief. Her heart, which had been pounding moments ago, now felt like it might burst from her chest. She couldn't tear her gaze away from Alex, who was looking at her with such intensity it made her knees weak.

Is this really happening? Lottie thought, her mind struggling to process the enormity of the moment. The man she'd fallen for, the reclusive rock legend who'd stolen her heart, had just declared his love for her in front of hundreds of people.

She felt a rush of emotions - joy, love, and a hint of fear at the magnitude of it all. The vinyl records lining the walls of **The Velvet Room** seemed to spin in her peripheral vision, a dizzying kaleidoscope of colors and memories.

Alex strummed the chords on his electric guitar in rhythm to the roar of applause from the crowd, and the drum beat steadily. His voice, low and velvety, sang the first words to his number-one song.

Hollow Reign was back…

THE END

acknowledgments

The Viper Room
Los Angeles, CA

'Purple Rain'
Vocals and Written by
Prince

Janis Joplin

Bob Dylan

Nirvana
Kurt Cobain

whispers of yesterday

An Age Gap Romance

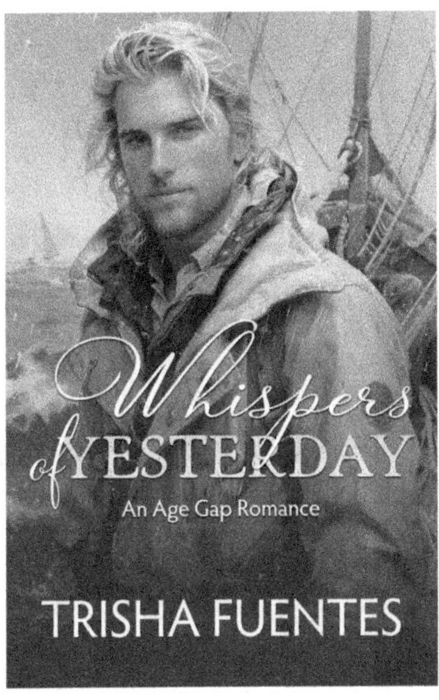

love's echoes whisper across the years in the scottish highlands.

Escape to the breathtaking beauty of the Scottish Highlands with **Whispers of Yesterday**, a heartwarming novel that explores the enduring power of love.

Evelyn O'Conner, a world-renowned architect in her prime, seeks solace on a remote Scottish island. There, amidst the rugged coastlines and ancient secrets, she encounters **Liam**

MacLeod, a brooding fisherman with a past as intriguing as the island itself.

Liam, younger by half, embodies the spirit of a life Evelyn once dreamt of. As they delve into conversations about dreams, regrets, and a shared passion for the island's history, a connection sparks, both unexpected and undeniable.

But can love truly bridge the gap between experience and youthful fire? Will the whispers of Evelyn's past silence the melody of their present?

Whispers of Yesterday is a captivating tale that proves love can bloom in the most unexpected places, challenging societal norms and reminding us that hearts know no age.

Embark on a heartwarming journey of love, loss, and second chances.

Available in

Ebook & Paperback

about trisha

Hey, it's Trish...

I'm a Romance Author of 39+ books, plus own a
Publishing House of 50+ Pen Name Authors.

I've been writing romance with a whole lot of heat lately.
I love to write fun, fast romances with witty leading ladies
getting that gorgeous, sexy, yet lovable guy that doesn't
take months to finish. Happily Ever After with a little bit
of love angst in between. Whether you yearn for
Historical or Modern, I always have a story for you!

Rejoice, Romance Reader...

For upcoming releases, book news, and other goodies, subscribe to my Newsletter!
https://bit.ly/49BR3UB

instagram.com/authortrish
amazon.com/Trisha-Fuentes/e/B002BME1MI
facebook.com/booksbyTrish
youtube.com/theardentartist

also by trisha fuentes

❊ Modern Romance ❊

A Sacrifice Play

Faded Dreams

Never Say Forever

* * *

❊ Historical ❊

The Anzan Heir

Magnet & Steele

The Relentless Rogue

One Starry Night

In The Moonlight With You

Captivating the Captain

The Merry Widow

Unrequited Love

The Summer Romance of the Duke

* Series *

HOLLINGER

Dare To Love - Book 1

A Matchless Match - Book 2

Arrogance & Conceit - Book 3

Impropriety - Book 4

SERVICE•DAUGHTER

The Steward's Daughter - Book 1

The Cook's Daughter - Book 2

The Curator's Daughter - Book 3

THUNDERBOLT

The Surprise Heir - Book 1

A Dance of Deception - Book 2

Win the Heart of a Duchess- Book 3

OBSESSION

Unsuitable Obsession - Part One

Broken Obsession - Part Two

ESCAPE

Swept Away - Book 1

Fire & Rescue - Book 2

The Domain King - Book 3

A G E • G A P • R O M A N C E

Whispers of Yesterday - Book 1

His Encore, Her Ecstasy - Book 2

Against the Wind - Book 3